SEND WAR IN OUR TIME, O LORD

Send War in Our Time, O Lord

a novel by
C. J. DRIVER

faber and faber

This edition first published in 2010
by Faber and Faber Ltd
Bloomsbury House, 74–77 Great Russell Street
London WC1B 3DA

Printed by Books on Demand GmbH, Norderstedt

All rights reserved
© C. J. Driver, 1970

The right of C. J. Driver to be identified as author of this work
has been asserted in accordance with Section 77 of the
Copyright, Designs and Patents Act 1988

This book is sold subject to the condition that it shall not, by way of
trade or otherwise, be lent, resold, hired out or otherwise circulated
without the publisher's prior consent in any form of binding or cover other than
that in which it is published and without a similar condition including this
condition being imposed on the subsequent purchaser

A CIP record for this book is available from the British Library

ISBN 978–0–571–25965–6

Our authorised representative in the EU for product safety is
Easy Access System Europe, Mustamäe tee 50, 10621 Tallinn, Estonia
gpsr.requests@easproject.com

for Ann

Author's Note

All the characters in this novel are fictitious; so are the Settlement of St. Joseph, the valley, the towns, and even the region. The country is obviously an actual one, though I have changed its geography, history and politics to suit my own purposes.

C.J.D.

Whether man die in his bed
Or the rifle knocks him dead,
A brief parting from those dear
Is the worst man has to fear.
Though grave-diggers' toil is long,
Sharp their spades, their muscles strong,
They but thrust their buried men
Back in the human mind again.

You that Mitchel's prayer have heard,
'Send war in our time, O Lord!' . . .

    W. B. YEATS, 'Under Ben Bulben'

(*Quoted with the permission of
M. B. Yeats and Macmillan & Co.*)

Contents

PART ONE	Your shadow at evening	*page* 11
PART TWO	Voices in an empty house	47
PART THREE	Immortality	127

PART ONE
Your shadow at evening

I

You have to look at the mountains first, for in that flat and circular land they are like the edge of the world itself, not high, oh no not high, but there, palpable almost, despite the distance, heavy, deeply ravined, thick with boulders which seem to hover for ever on the edge of falling without ever falling. They look dangerous, the mountains, yet they are not unexpected, for they seem like a magnified reflection of the low hills that circle inwards into the valley; it must have been a lake once, this valley—though a lake is almost unimaginable now—and when the water gradually went down, it left in each age a rim of dried earth that became rock and then hills, perhaps thick with woods once, but naked now, hardly covered by the earth, like the ridges of skin over the muscles on the back of a sleeping animal. Circle upon circle, the hills work their way into the centre of the valley and there, right in the middle, like a passive reflection of the troubled perimeter, is a circle of buildings which surrounds a last dust-bowl.

Circles—the circles of the sky, of the mountains, of the hills, of the buildings, of the central arena; and dust too—dust that makes the winds seem visible, dust that trails for miles behind each motor-car that comes down through the mountains and over the low hills on the road that leads to the settlement, dust that puffs and pants with every step you take. Circles and dust.

II

As she climbed out of the car, Mrs. Allen noticed, with a shudder, that her hands were already grimy. The train had of course been dirty; but she had washed her face and hands carefully before arriving in Verderdorp station—she had wanted to make a good impression on the Superintendent of the settlement, for he had written to say that he would meet her train so that they could discuss her work before she arrived at the settlement. Not that he seemed to remember that, she thought; and not that she need to have bothered to wash and put on a clean dress—he would not have noticed if she had come in dungarees; he had not even offered to shake hands with her, had barely said How do you do, Mrs. Allen, before he had grabbed two of her suitcases and, leaving her to manage the others, had walked (in front of her!) to the car. And he had hardly said a word to her in the car; and how hot it had been—he had kept the windows wound up, so that the car smelt. After a mile or two she had asked if she might open the window next to her; and he had still said nothing, had simply nodded, and had opened his own too. Well, even if he was going to be like that to her, she would still go on being herself; and no sooner had she thought that than it was necessary to admit that he might have been right to keep the windows of the car closed, for having them open meant that the dust swirled in in thick clouds. How on earth, she wondered, would it be possible to keep herself clean, much less to keep the settlement, even the wards of the hospital, clean. Why, the dust lay as thick on everything as dew would on grass in the early morning.

She stood by the side of the car, looking around her at the settlement, not allowing her gaze to go beyond the buildings to the hills or the mountains through which she had just been driven. The place was not at all what she had imagined it would be; she had known that this was a dry land, but she had expected some trees at least, and perhaps aloes and shrubs and even some wild flowers; but there seemed to be nothing at all here, just dusty ground and a few red rocks and occasional scraggly bushes —and she had expected white, brilliant, sun-baked buildings, not these mainly grey-brown huts—and, she admitted to herself, she had expected some kind of welcome; after all, they had been without a Matron for nearly eighteen months now—and that was hardly surprising, for only someone like herself with some kind of moral stake in the place would have been prepared to come to this run-down settlement. But the people she could see among the buildings showed not the slightest interest in her arrival; they went about their business as if nothing unusual were happening.

* * *

By now, the African man who had been up a ladder painting the outside of one of the houses as the car arrived, had come running over the dust-bowl and had managed to get her cases out of the boot of the car and the various packages from the back seat. He left the packages on top of the biggest of the cases, tucked the smallest case under his arm, picked up two others, and staggered off with them towards what Mrs. Allen guessed must be the Matron's quarters, a small red-brick cottage built near what was obviously the hospital. Mr. Schwartz, the Superintendent, picked one of the parcels off the large suitcase and, without saying a word to her, started off after the African. Mrs. Allen held back for a moment or two, just long enough, she thought, to show the man that she noticed how uncouth his behaviour was, and then walked through the dust after him.

When she caught up with him, they walked in silence for a few yards; then, so suddenly that she was for a moment almost frightened, Mr. Schwartz said, without turning to look at her, "We haven't had decent rain for more than eight months now, Mrs. Allen. That's why the dust is so bad."

"What do you do for water?" she asked.

"There's a pipe-line from the Verderdorp reservoir and we have our own bore-hole," he said, still without looking at her. He gestured towards the west of the settlement from where came the monotonous clank clank of a one-stroke engine. Mrs. Allen looked but could not see.

"But isn't the pipe-line water very expensive?" she asked. "I mean, it has to come from so far away."

"No, it does not. The reservoir for Verderdorp is up there in the mountains." Again he gestured away, but now Mrs. Allen did not try to see if there was anything to be seen. "The reservoir used to be for Verderdorp only, but then the Government put in a special pipe-line to the settlement." The last he said as if he were closing the conversation, as if he had already said too much; and now he walked a little quicker, so that Mrs. Allen had to lengthen her stride to keep up with him. But she understood; perhaps that is why he is being so curt to me, she thought—perhaps he is expecting me to be an enemy. It would be natural, of course, for him to think that; she had forgotten that there might be that tension still. He was the Superintendent appointed by the Government; she had got the job because of her husband's connection with the settlement as it had been before the Government had insisted on taking over the bulk of control of all mission settlement in African areas, some twenty-five years before. Some of the churches had, of course, simply given up all their mission settlements; but the Anglicans had decided that they must render unto Caesar what he demanded, though they decided only after heart-searching and doubt. She could even remember one of the phrases from the angry letter which Terry had written to the *Chronicle* when the Act had been passed: "As grandson of the founder of the famous Settlement of St. Joseph," he had written, "I think I can say that he would have taken arms to oppose the enforcement of this pernicious Act." But, of course, as even hot-headed Terry had been forced to admit, that would have been useless; the Church had no power to stand against the machinery of the Government. But if Mr. Schwartz wanted to continue the old feud, if he wanted to keep that barrier between them, why then she knew where she stood; oh, there was no doubt about that, at any rate—she belonged to the party of the Church, as Terry had done. That, of course, was why she had never been here before—even Terry had kept away from the settlement for more than twenty years. He had talked about bringing her here when they were first married, but the children had come so quickly and Terry and she had been so busy at the school that they had not managed to. After the Act, of course, they had resolved not to go near the settlement, and it hadn't been until three years ago that Terry had visited it again; that had been just after the first Government Superintendent, the ghastly Dr. Luxson, they had called him, had retired and before Mr. Schwartz had come. She had wanted very much to come with Terry, but one of them had to stay behind, because that holidays there had been nobody but them to look after the school and the host of servants. Well, at least she was here now, she thought—to do what had to be done.

The African man had put her cases down in the small hall of the cottage; and, as he was crossing the dust-bowl, back to fetch the other cases, Mr. Schwartz said to her, "I think that you will find everything in your quarters in order, Mrs. Allen. I will leave you now, and will call for you again at five minutes to seven," and without waiting for a reply, turned to walk away.

Mrs. Allen's "Where are you going, Mr. Schwartz?" stopped him. He turned back to her, slightly puzzled, as if he expected her to continue. But when she did not, he was forced to reply:

"I am going to take this parcel to deliver it," he said, and then added, "to the school."

"May I come with you?"

"Don't you want to wash and to change?"

"To tell the truth," she said, and now she was making a conscious effort to be and to sound friendly towards him, "to tell the truth, I am far too excited about being here at last to want to stay in my room. I would like to see the school, if you don't mind my coming with you."

"Of course," said Mr. Schwartz, and waited for her while she crossed the few yards of dust between them. After they had walked a part of the way across the dust-bowl in silence, he spoke again: "I have to deliver these maps—" and he gestured with the parcel—"to the native school teacher. I bought them on the way to fetching you . . . I am always prepared," he went on, "to do errands for the people of the settlement—including you now, of course—when I go to town. Dr. Redman does not go often and you don't have a motor, of course . . ." and his voice tailed off, as if he were afraid that he was saying something that she would not understand. Why, thought Mrs Allen, he's beginning to be quite talkative; perhaps he is responding to my attempt at friendliness, or perhaps he is feeling ashamed of having treated me so rudely until now; after all, living out here he probably feels very isolated—and so has grown to distrust meeting new people. That at least she could understand: Terry and she had always been a little like that, and one of the reasons for her taking the job here had been so that she would be able to be alone, would be able to be her developed self, her widowed self, but herself, not just her children's mother, possessed by the past although working in the present and for the present. So she tried to continue the conversation which he seemed to have started; but once again the curtness of his replies and his unwillingness or inability to look at her when he spoke to her thwarted her attempts.

The school lay almost exactly across the dust-bowl from the Matron's cottage. As they walked, their feet scuffing up small eddies of dust. Mrs. Allen tried to notice things—you noticed the circle of the buildings, of course: that was a relic of the days when the settlement had been fortified—you noticed how wide the circle was: that was originally so that you could herd all the goats and cattle of the tribesmen of the valley into the protection of the settlement in a time of trouble—you noticed that the fields around the settlement were so eroded that it was a wonder that anything grew there at all—and you noticed the long shadows that swept along beside you, as if each of you were accompanied by someone else—and always there was the dust, blinding you, choking you, so that even if you wanted to speak, your voice would not be your own.

The Superintendent knocked at the door of a small cottage, really only a brick hut, next to the school. No one answered. He knocked again and, while he was still knocking, a small boy came out of the school and called to them, "The teacher is here." But before they reached the school, the teacher came out, carrying a blue exercise book; he was very thin, very tall, much darker skinned than any of the Africans Mrs. Allen had seen while they were crossing the dust-bowl. Standing next to the Superintendent he was fully a head taller than him—and Mr. Schwartz is not a particularly small man, thought Mrs. Allen.

"This is the native school teacher, Johannes Simbele," Mr. Schwartz introduced him; Mrs. Allen smiled at him and reached out to shake hands with him but, deliberately it seemed, he ignored her hand and bowed, very coldly, very formally. Without speaking, the Superintendent handed him the parcel.

"Thank you," said Simbele. "These will be most useful for my Geography classes," and, bowing to Mrs. Allen again, he turned away. But she would not have this, she thought; the people in the settlement seemed to make a policy of this polite, formal unfriendliness—that wasn't what she had come for; she had come here to work, to understand; and the sooner she began to break down the barriers of formality, the better.

"Mr. Simbele," she called him back. "I would very much like to see your school, if you would not mind showing me."

Again the formal bow: and then he said, "It is not my school; it is the school of the settlement. If you wish, and the Superintendent does not mind, I shall show you the school room," and he looked at Mr. Schwartz, not at all as if asking for permission, but as if challenging him.

Looking at his watch, Mr. Schwartz said, "Mrs. Allen, it is now ten minutes to seven. Staff supper is at seven promptly. I think that it would be better if you saw the school tomorrow, when you can ask questions at your leisure. If you will excuse us, Johannes . . ."

Again the bow; and now, at last, a smile—but so mocking, so . . . almost inhuman, thought Mrs. Allen, as if we were machines who had done exactly what machines should do, as if he were a scientist who watched an experiment. But she would not be daunted; she would not allow herself to see the challenge; so she took a step forward, and put out a hand again, this time in such a way that Simbele was forced to shake it, and said, "I look forward to tomorrow, then," and turned away with the Superintendent. But after she had walked a yard or two, she turned again, back to Simbele, about to say something. He was not looking after them, but was staring at his hand, the hand which she had shaken, had insisted on shaking, almost as if, she thought, it had somehow been dirtied, as if it were stained, as if he wished he could cut it off. She had turned back to say, You know, Mr. Simbele, my husband was a teacher too; I have lived all my married life in schools: but how could she say that now, having seen that look? What could she say? Simbele was looking at her now, looking straight at her, and he did not bother to conceal his loathing.

As she turned away from him again, she felt suddenly as if

the dust were choking her; there was so much hate there, where she had expected to find love. The Superintendent hated her: why? Because she came from the side opposed to the Government. Was that enough to cause hate? Simbele hated her: why? She could only suppose because she was white. Was that cause for hate either? She felt suddenly helpless; and what was worse, abandoned—for the first time since her husband's death she felt she was nowhere near him; she was lost, the chain of love had broken. O Terry, Terry, she cried to herself: what can I do? How can I cope without you?

But she allowed herself despair for only a moment. The settlement was too much of her imagined past, too much of her hope, for her to allow herself despair. The people living here would not matter all that much; because she was living with the past, at least in the sense that she was working out the past. This was where she would make her wifehood perfect; Terry would always be with her, because this was the place of his ancestral grave; why, only half a mile away, up there on the hillside, lay the grave of the founder of the Allen family, the founder of this settlement, the world-famous Doctor Timothy Xavier Allen, the enormous, larger-than-life hunter turned doctor and then missionary, one of the first men to see that the way to men's souls lay through proper care of their bodies, the champion of the Africans against the encroachment of the white settlers—this was the model of man's goodness to man. This was the foundation Terry had built his life on; and this was why she had come here. Why should she care that a man like Simbele hated her for no good reason? She had her own strength and the strength of her husband and the strength of all the dead Allens to support her.

Mr. Schwartz was talking to her: she had not heard him, so deeply was she immersed in her own thoughts. "Sorry," she said, "I didn't hear what you said. I was thinking of something else."

"I said that you will of course know all about Dr. Redman, whom you will be meeting at supper."

"Yes, I have heard of him," she replied. "I haven't of course met him before."

"We were all very grateful to your husband for finding us a doctor," he said; but he spoke without real warmth, and again she wondered if he were resenting the fact that it had been an Allen who had helped the settlement. For Terry had been wonderful about that; when he had visited the settlement three years before, one of the things that he had discovered was that it had been without a qualified doctor for nearly eight months, despite advertisements, despite appeals by both the Church and by the Department of National Health and Welfare. Immediately on his return to the school, he had set about finding someone; he had written to various friends, had paid for an advertisement in the *Chronicle*, and had written personally to the heads of all the medical schools in the country. Finally, the dean of the medical school of the University of Cape Town had written to say that he had persuaded a young Jewish houseman to do the job for a few years, despite the conditions of work and the appallingly low salary which was offered by the Church. That had been Dr. Redman; and, although they were sorry that the doctor wasn't a Christian—as after all it was a Church appointment—it seemed, from all Terry heard, that he had been a great success at the settlement, persuading a wealthy local resident to refit the surgery, training three competent African women as ward nurses, and even persuading the Government to help the settlement set up a fund for building a proper new maternity ward. She was looking forward to meeting him; he, at least, would be an ally.

III

Later that night, when all the lights in the white people's quarters were out, Simbele the schoolteacher left his hut, very quietly, and cut away from the settlement for a few hundred yards, to just below the immediate circle of hills; he followed the circle half-way round before crossing the hills and setting off on the two-hour walk that would take him to the foot of the mountains to the south of the settlement. On his back he carried a large and heavily laden haversack. He would have two hours when he got there and there would be two hours walking to get him back again, with luck before sun-rise; but the walking back would be easier without the burden of the full haversack. Then he would have three hours for washing himself and sleeping, before he started teaching next morning. But he would be able to sleep for a couple of hours next afternoon; and anyway he was getting used to this occasional nightly stint; and anyway the weariness was good—it gave you less time to think.

You didn't want too much time for thinking now; you simply wanted time to pass, until you were ready. It was better not to think; you had eventually to reach that stage where only what had to be done mattered. Before, he had understood the purpose; now, he cared only for the action—it was almost as if everything but the weight of the purpose had disappeared; there was nothing else left now—but because you had started on this road, you kept on it. If you needed to, you could always leave it; he'd left it before, after all. But now he was tired of leaving; he was going to stay on this road, this all-road, until he reached an end. There was a time when you were sure—

when you had been sure, he corrected himself; now there was only a vague memory of certainty, like a dream you think you may have dreamed but can't be sure of—you just thought that you had dreamed some time. When certainty disappeared, as it was bound to, you could simply only remember that you had once been sure, and stick to the same road. It grew darker every time; but you knew the road, and you followed it.

Anyway, they were expecting him; they needed the food he carried in the haversack; and he had managed to get the map they needed—that had been quite clever, the getting of those maps; he had told the Superintendent he needed the maps, three large-scale ordnance maps of the region, for teaching the pupils local Geography. The Superintendent had got them from the local bookshop for him when he went to fetch the new woman; one he had put on the wall of the main classroom; one was in his desk; one was in his haversack. Nobody would miss it; and if the police ever found this one, no-one would suspect the Superintendent of having supplied it. Yes, that had been quite clever; he smiled to himself, the same mocking smile that Mrs. Allen had seen that afternoon.

How he despised that woman, he thought—despised and distrusted her, right from the first moment, all that eagerness, that open-handedness, that pretence at respect. "Mr. Simbele," she said; "Johannes", said the Superintendent, and in a way he preferred the second, because at least you knew then that there was no pretence, that he had no feeling for you except as an overgrown child. Mr. Simbele! Oh that was fine, fine; but if you put it to the test, if you tried to see if the need to be loved included the ability to love, you always found an emptiness, a nothing, a polite nothing. He was a teacher, he was respectable, he dressed like a European, so she called him Mr. Simbele and wanted to shake hands with him, wanted to "treat him like a white man". Well, he was not a white man, he was black, he was as black as any farm labourer, as any convict, and he wanted to be treated as black. There were some things that were simple: that was one of them, and you simply accepted those. There were other things that were much more complicated; it was out of those that you grew, that you went on growing.

The straps of the haversack were biting into his shoulders; he eased the weight by tugging at the straps, but did not slow down. Very soon now he would have to begin the detour that would take him safely around the Viljoen farm and their barking dogs; and then he would just keep going, straight towards the mountains that lay shadowy in the distance before him.

IV

Mrs. Allen woke very early next morning; she had woken once during the night, had woken herself by an effort of will to escape from a terrible dream—but the trouble was that even in the morning she remembered it, for, from the earliest days of their marriage, she had grown into a habit of telling her dreams to Terry when she woke in the morning. He had been a bad sleeper, and he used, when they had first married, to have terrible nightmares, would wake screaming and sweating, clutching her for protection, like a child seeking its mother. Strange that had been, for he had needed so little mothering in most ways, had usually in those days been almost fiercely independent of her; and he would never tell her what his nightmares had been about, or he could not tell her. So she used to tell him about her dreams, would sometimes even make them up, or would embroider what she remembered of them, to help him emerge from the horror of his own; and in some strange way, a way that was mysterious to both of them, she had slowly been able to release him from his nightmares by taking them upon herself, as if she were dreaming them for him, so that she would wake up screaming herself and would have to seek the protection of his body, and would, next morning, weep out her terrible dream which was really his dream.

This morning, even before she opened her eyes, she knew where she was—and for the first time since Terry had died she did not turn over in the bed in the fond hope that everything, every single thing, might have been a bad dream—that he would be lying, fast asleep, in the bed next to hers and that she would be able to tell him what she had dreamed. Now she had no need to look; he would not be there, she knew, but in a way he was there, with her. After all, this place was Allen territory, for, no matter who had superficial control of it, it would not have been there if it had not been for the Allens. Where so much of the family dream was, Terry was too; she was sure of that. Oh, he wasn't there as a ghost or even a spirit; her religious feeling was more sophisticated than that, but he was there as a part of his ancestral delight and ancestral burden. He was dead, yes, but he survived; he survived in the past, because of his family; he survived in the present, because of what he had done—and because of their love; and he would survive into the future, because of her love; and not static love either, because it was to be demonstrated, here in the settlement—because hadn't he said to her, after his last visit there, and before he had known that he was dying, that as soon as he could find someone competent enough to take over his own school he would like to go back to the settlement permanently, to spend the last years of his life working and teaching there? But no one competent enough had turned up; and then death had come; and now she was here alone, to complete for both of them what he had wanted to complete.

She sat up in bed and pulled the blankets up over her knees, then closed her eyes and, as if Terry could actually hear, she whispered out the dream. He would have laughed gently at parts of it, she knew; he would have explained parts of it, she knew; he would have comforted her. Yet though she knew that he could not actually hear, the very act of whispering aloud as if he were listening was enough to comfort her. When she finished, she opened her eyes again: the dream had gone away, had disappeared into the darkness of her mind, had left her free again. The sun was up; there was a small dawn wind tugging at the curtains drawn over the open windows; it was time for her to begin her work, the work she was doing both for Terry and for herself.

But before she started, there was one thing to be done first, a pilgrimage to be made. She got up, washed, dressed, left her cottage, looked into the main kitchen to see what time staff breakfast was, and, discovering that it was not until eight, set off.

Although it was only half past six, the sun was well up; the stillness of dawn was disturbed by the wind picking and puffing the dust between the buildings of the settlement. A few children were playing over on the other side of the settlement, among the huts of the Africans; there was a man washing himself outside one of the huts, scooping water from a bucket over his head and arms; far away to the east of the settlement, there was a single man walking towards the huts; she shaded her eyes against the early glare of the sun, but she could not distinguish him. What was he doing, she wondered idly; to be out so early, that was strange—but he was probably some young man returning from one of the nearby farms. She turned round again and looked up the slight rise in front of her; slowly she walked along the winding goat-path that led from the staff quarters, past the hospital wards, and then up the incline to where the crosses of the cemetery threw little early shadows yards over the ground.

The grave, though it was marked in stone, wasn't ostentatious; she hadn't expected it to be, but for a moment or two she could not spot it. Once you did, though, she thought, you couldn't help realizing that it was the vital grave there; it wasn't even central and the head-stone was no higher than some of the others; but you could feel that it was especial. Still, there was no hurry; she knew what she wanted to see, so she could afford to walk slowly between the other graves, noting the names and the dates—"Jeremy Alfred Dirkson, 1905–1961, who served this community for twenty years as a devoted and loving teacher", "Peter David Williamson, 1896–1925, doctor of medicine, and servant of God Almighty", "Martha Gwendolyn MacArthur, d. 1934, for fifteen years Matron of this Settlement. May she rest in the peace of Heaven", and then the grave of another matron, who had been here only three years. The graves of children, servants, missionaries; most of the Africans had wooden crosses—the doctors, the priests, the farmers, the matrons, they had stone; but everything was simple, everything was in what Mrs. Allen thought the best possible taste—orderly, but informal. And there was the one she had come to see: "Timothy Xavier Allen, b. 1825, d. 1876, Beloved Missionary and Healer, Founder of St. Joseph's Settlement". She hardly needed to look at the inscription; she knew it already. Hadn't she promised Terry that she would have on his grave simply "Terry Xavier Allen, b. 1919. d. 1972, Teacher". That had been all. That was all. That was what mattered—the name and the work; he had even thought of leaving the dates out.

Well, there it was. There he was. He was the first one, the first one who mattered, anyway; what a man he must have been, she thought, to have so consumed her husband's imagination. What he had done had been the model always for Terry, the same love for the weak and the poor, the same hatred of injustice, the same arrogance of certainty that went somehow with the humility of self-doubt, the same ability to face the worst that the world could offer with pride and with scorn. She looked up now from the grave to the rise of the hill in front of her, and on to the mountains; she was smiling as if she were waiting for someone to appear. It was a long way to walk to the mountains, where the dead lay—that was something Terry had told her, a remembrance from the stories of his childhood. Here, he was close; yes, he was close, he was nearly there, she was nearly with him. Yes, she had been right to come here, for his presence here was more real even than at the school where they had lived all of their married lives.

Suddenly, from behind her, came, like the cawing of a savage crow, a high-pitched cackle of a laugh. In her fright, Mrs. Allen could not help herself; she stepped forward on to the grave, crying out as she did so and half-flinging herself around to face whatever it was behind her. The laugh, if it could be called that, came from a very small, very old, very dirty black man, who must have walked up the earth path behind her, quietly so that she could not hear him.

"What do you want?" she asked, angry that she had been so nervy. Again the old man laughed that screaming, almost girlishly high-pitched, cawing laugh.

"Stop it," Mrs. Allen said, and as she did so, realized with horror that she was still standing on the grave. She stepped off it again as quickly as she could, on to the path the other side. The old man came, with the slow short steps of the very old, around the grave towards her and, almost involuntarily, Mrs. Allen backed away.

"What do you want?" she asked again, still backing away. The old man stopped and, still looking at her, fumbled inside the ancient and over-sized coat which he wore. To her amazement he produced from somewhere inside the coat a small bunch of white Barberton daisies which, although he did not take his eyes off her, he laid down at the foot of the head-stone of Dr. Allen's grave. Slowly he stood up again. Again he laughed, turned away and began to make his slow progress across the cemetery. After a moment or two, Mrs. Allen called out, "What's your name?" and when he did not answer, again, "What's your name? Old man, what is your name?" But he did not turn. Perhaps he can't hear, thought Mrs. Allen; and, almost to her own surprise, she began to follow him across the cemetery. He moved so slowly that it seemed to take a very long time, but eventually he got to what was obviously the newer part of the cemetery. The old man turned now to see her following him and, again cackling, he pointed an arthritic forefinger at the piled mound of a new grave; and then, seeming to forget her again, he picked up in his clawed and crooked hands a spade and began to dig in short jabbing scratches at the dusty ground next to the new grave; every few minutes he punctuated his digging with a senile cackle of laughter. How long it must take him to dig each new grave, Mrs. Allen thought; and she laughed at the thought, though her laugh was as much a shudder as anything. All the optimism of her earlier mood had gone now and she returned to the terror of the dream; but walking back she re-created the mood and remembered that Terry was still there with her, that he would always be there.

At breakfast, half an hour later, she asked Dr. Redman about the old man she had seen in the cemetery. "Oh, that's old Joseph," he answered. "Did you see him? An advanced case of senile decay. Did he frighten you?" and, ignoring Mrs. Allen's quick "No", went on, "The other Africans are terrified of him. They seem to think he's a sort of personification of the devil." He laughed and then rubbed his hand over his face—he's looking very tired, thought Mrs. Allen; he must have been working late last night—he'd told her that he was trying to keep up with some of the latest research in his own particular field of the treatment of diseases of malnutrition. She hadn't liked him very much the night before; he had seemed too conceited, too boastful—and there was something else there that she didn't like but that she was not sure she could identify, some way of looking at her, almost, she had thought, as if he were . . . well, thinking obscene thoughts about her. She had pushed the reaction out of her mind: it was ridiculous, it was probably only some peculiar caste of the face—after all, she was old enough to be his mother.

Now, interested in what he said about the old man, she asked, "Do you know how old he is, old Joseph I mean?"

The Superintendent, who had sat silent through the meal so far, replied for Redman. "I've heard it said," he answered, "that Old Joseph was here in the days when Dr. Allen was still alive. I doubt if it is true."

"It may be," said Redman. "He could well be about that old. It's so difficult to tell, of course." He looked quizzically at Mrs. Allen, laughed, and said, "Actually, I've heard it said that he is in fact an off-spring of the original Dr. Allen—one of his bastards. I don't know whether it's true, of course."

Mrs. Allen looked at him in disgust. "What a revolting thing to say," she said carefully. "Everything I've read from Dr. Allen's papers—my husband had the full collection, you know—makes it clear that he adored his wife."

Smilingly, Dr. Redman said, "But she was dead by the time he came here, wasn't she?"

"Yes, she was—but he still adored her and the suggestion that he was immoral is unthinkable." She was beginning to be angry with this over-confident and impertinent young man; she tried hard not to be, for she did not want to dislike him: but, really, he was being very silly. So she tried to change the conversation slightly—"I saw old Joseph putting flowers on Dr. Allen's grave," she said.

"Oh yes, he does that every day," said Redman. "Does that lend credence to the story, do you think? Of old Joseph being the bastard of Dr. Allen, I mean?"

Mrs. Allen pushed her chair back from the table. "Really, Doctor," she said, emphasizing his title to show that she was being formal, "I would be grateful if you would spare me these speculations about my husband's grandfather."

He grinned at her and then at the silent Superintendent. "Sorry," he said. "I forgot. But," he continued, "he is a frightening old man. I always react like a Catholic whenever I come near him—I find myself wanting to make a swift cross to keep his influence off me. Don't you find that, Mr. Schwartz?" he asked, though the tone of his voice made it clear that he did not want an answer; he was simply making some kind of sarcastic gesture at the Superintendent.

But the Superintendent answered quite seriously. "No, I see

no reason to do that under any circumstances." Then, having killed Redman's jibe at him, he looked at his watch. "Well, Mrs. Allen, if you have finished your breakfast, perhaps it is time that I showed you what your duties are."

"Of course," said Mrs. Allen and stood up. Now was the time to work; there would be time for thoughts later.

V

Mrs. Allen was an ordinary woman—or so she always said; it was her husband who was extraordinary. So, when he died, it seemed almost that, mixed in with the extraordinary grief she felt, there was a sort of proud relief as well; not at all relief that she was free of him, for she knew that she would never, not for a moment, exist as anything but his widow, just as she had been, since the moment of their marriage, nothing but his wife. No, the relief she felt was the relief that now she would be able to perfect her wifehood, that she would not have the sense of not being quite able to keep up with him, simply because the actual job of being his wife had involved her in so many things that were not essential to her concept of wifehood. Wife and now widow, that was what made her special in her own eyes; nothing in her own right, she had existed only to be his wife; now she was only his widow. Everything that she did now was part of that vision of herself. She existed now to serve his memory.

She had known this even before the funeral; she had known this as soon as the doctor had told her that Terry was dying. He wasn't an old man, not at all an old man, but he hadn't been afraid to die. And she had believed him, not simply because he told her, but because she knew that he, of all people, would not be afraid. Of course, he had died well—in agony (and she remembered and shut her mind to those last months) but well, refusing more drugs than were absolutely necessary to keep him sane, insisting, right at the end, that he wanted rather agonized consciousness than the peace of the drugs which the doctor was urging him to accept.

If he hadn't been afraid to die, no more must she be afraid to live. He had said that to her early on in his illness, when for the only time she had broken down and confessed her own despair. Of course, the women in her family lived to be old; she had been married to him for twenty-eight years: yes, that was it, twenty when he had married her, twenty-eight years of marriage, and now it was perfectly likely that she would live twenty-eight years more. Seventy-six! Why, that was, in her family, young; her mother, for instance, had died not of old age, but in a street accident, and she had been perfectly capable at eighty-seven. Terry had known that; he was dying at fifty-three, but she would have at least as long to live as his widow as she had been his wife.

Before him, what had she been? She had been little more than a schoolgirl, she remembered, a schoolgirl from a narrow life in one street in a small town, a silly, nervy girl, afraid of the dark, of heights, of strangers—and he had made her whole world, he had been lover, husband, father, ancestor almost, child almost; for the children had been so like him, not only in the way they looked but in the way they were, the way they spoke, thought, felt. It was almost as if Terry himself had created her—before him she had been nothing, under his love and guidance she had become a person, and now that he was dead she would not be afraid.

You must never be afraid again, he had said to her once; and he had said again that she mustn't be afraid before he went into that last haze of drugs; and he hadn't meant that she should suddenly become flighty, should become a travelling widow, staying three months in a hotel by the sea, three with her daughter, three with her son in England, and three travelling. No, he had meant that she must work. Living meant working. Hadn't he died partly because he had always over-worked himself? The specialist had said that: "He has the constitution of a much older man than he is," he had told Mrs Allen. "He could not fight this off even if we could treat it." So, before the funeral even, she had written to the Bishop of the Diocese of Northern Tswanaland and had asked if there was by any chance a post at the Settlement of St. Joseph which might be suitable for a middle-aged lady of no particular qualifications, except the family connection and enthusiasm. Well, of course, unless she was to live on her children's charity, she had needed the money too, because she and Terry had always been poor, even at the end. But it wasn't simply money; she could have earned more money by going as matron to a boarding school—and she wouldn't have had any trouble getting a post like that, not with Terry's reputation to back her application. She could have been more comfortable living with her daughter in Johannesburg or her son in England; but she wanted Caroline and Peter to have complete independence or, perhaps, she admitted to herself, she still thought of herself as more a wife than a mother and so wanted to live her own life, her own widowhood. Anyway, she was still young; she wanted to work.

In the meantime, there had been the funeral; the clearing of the school house; the presentation of Terry's collection of Africana, including the priceless Allen papers, to the University library; the storage of the valuable furniture, the sale of the rest; the discussions about the estate with the bank manager and her son Peter, who had come especially from England for the funeral; the distribution of Terry's wardrobe to the poor in the local township; and all the time, grief hovered like a vulture over her, hovering, hovering in a wide-winged sweeping: so she must work or go mad.

What they demanded of her at the settlement was not, in fact, all that rigorous. Over the years its size had decreased drastically; in the great days of Dr. Allen there had been over a thousand people living there—but the demands of the towns, the poverty of the area, the regular and terrifying droughts, had all helped to drive people away from the settlement. Now, there were only a few more than two hundred people living there. Some of the men worked as casual labourers on local farms but most of them were away for long spells, working in the phosphate and copper mines to the east, in the gold mines of the Free State, in the factories of the Witwatersrand, in the homes of the rich white people in the towns. A few came back, for extended holidays until their savings ran out, or for short visits to their wives and children, or because they were too ill to cope with the demands of the mines and the towns. The lands of the settlement were worked by the women and the old men; the goats and the few scrawny cows were shepherded by the very young and the very old.

Each family on the settlement paid ten shillings a month to live there. In return they got a brick hut and weekly rations of meal and meat and every child a glass of milk a day. They got free medical attention and the children got free schooling. The profits from what little of its farm-produce the settlement could sell—the skins of goats, the occasional surplus of mealie meal—went into a communal fund which was administered by a committee of the people living there, advised by the Superintendent, and which was meant to be spent on new buildings and better living conditions, but which in fact had to be spent on maintaining the old buildings. The salary of the Superintendent was paid by the Government, the salaries of the doctor, matron, and teacher by the Church. Once, there had been an agricultural officer too; but the droughts had been so bad for so many years that it was hardly worthwhile employing one, even if one could have been found. So the people themselves saw to the lands and the crops. Once a week, the Anglican priest from Verderdorp visited the settlement and held a service in the open arena between the buildings; there wasn't a church at the settlement—that had been one of Dr. Allen's most original ideas. "Our church," he had maintained, "will be in the hearts and minds of our people; we shall not need bricks and mortar to worship a living God." He had been accused of heresy for that, Mrs. Allen remembered—but who could touch him out here then? And now, even if they had wanted a church, there would not have been the money to build it.

In short, when Dr. Allen had founded the settlement, it had been revolutionary. Now, thought Mrs. Allen, it was simply a run-down Mission, no different from thousands of others in a hundred poor countries all over the world. Terry had known that; and that was one of his reasons for wanting to return; he had wanted to re-create the original vitality of the place, to show what could still be done by the principles of community and charity. That's really what my work is going to be, thought Mrs. Allen; I won't be able to say that, but once I have mastered my own immediate job, I shall set about re-creating what my husband's family tried to create.

Her immediate work involved three main things: the supervision of the nurses, the supervision of the staff kitchen and living quarters, and general supervision of the tidiness and cleanliness of the settlement. She sorted out the first of these jobs in a fortnight; she sacked one of the nurses whom she discovered was pilfering food and medical supplies from the hospital; she and Dr. Redman interviewed three young African women for the vacant job and chose one, the youngest and, as it happened, the prettiest, Temana Peters—she would, as Mrs. Allen said, be easier to train in habits of cleanliness than older women; Mrs. Allen spent hours with the nurses making an inventory of everything in the hospital, and marking every sheet, pillow-case, blanket, towel, even every bandage, with the initials of the settlement, S.J.S.; she asked the Superintendent to buy a new lock for the cupboards in the dispensary and got Dr. Redman to fit them for her—one key she kept herself, on the big bunch that was hung just inside the kitchen door in her cottage, and one she gave to Dr. Redman. Then she persuaded Dr. Redman to appoint the oldest of the nurses, Mrs. Mbele, as sister and herself gave her detailed instructions of what her duties were—that released three hours of her working day, for now she had only to supervise one sister, rather than three nurses. She sacked the slattern who cooked meals for the staff and the hospital and replaced her with an old man who had once been assistant cook in a large hotel in Johannesburg; the food improved out of all recognition. Mrs. Allen then got down on her hands and knees to demonstrate to the cleaning women how floors should be scrubbed properly. She bribed six of the older children to spend half an hour every morning and afternoon sprinkling water over the central dust-bowl so that, for part of the day at least, the settlement was free of the cloying, clinging clouds of dust. She persuaded the Superintendent to move the rubbish dump farther away from the camp and she herself supervised all the men in the camp one Sunday while they dug a deep pit to bury the rubbish in. She set up, in the living-room of her own house, a créche for all the children too young to be left alone; she appointed two of the older women to act as créche mothers and saw to it that the young mothers thus released got out into the fields to help with the hoeing. She paid young Petrus, Sister Mbele's son, to build her a rockery outside her cottage and she planted succulents and aloes herself. Once she even went out into the fields herself, dressed in her oldest clothes, and for two hours hoed the crops of mealie meal with the rest of the African women; but since the Superintendent was for once vehement and told her that if she ever did anything like that again he would see to it that she was sacked immediately and since her hands were so blistered that she had to keep them bandaged for a week and her back so sore that for two days she could hardly walk, she decided that it was not worth fighting a large-scale battle over that particular issue.

Deliberately, Mrs. Allen cut herself off from the outside world. There was no point in reading the newspapers anyway; by the time they got to the settlement they were three days old.

She made an effort at first to listen to the news every morning on the portable radio which Caroline and Charles had given her for Christmas, but what was said was so crooked that it was hardly worth listening to, so she decided to give that up too. Of course, she wrote to her children every week, to Peter in England on Wednesdays and to Caroline on Sundays; but she knew that she had got into a muddle over what she had written to one and not the other, and Caroline told her, after three weeks of letters, that her mother had told her three times all about Dr. Redman and had still not said a word about the house she lived in. Caroline was very good about writing; she never missed a week, unless one of the children was ill. Peter was hopeless, of course; when he had first gone to England, he used to write often, but now that he was working so hard, he seldom wrote, sometimes not for three months at a time; then he would spend pounds sending a long cable saying that he was writing and a month later, longer sometimes, a letter would come at last. Peter was doing so well, she thought, yet she couldn't help feeling a little disappointed in him—not that he was lazy or a failure or anything like that, but she and Terry had sent him to England thinking that he would only be there a year or two and that he would then come, to put his talents to the best possible use. Instead, he had decided to settle there forever, to give up his country, for all its wrongs, and to stay where there were no big battles to be fought—and now he was in Market Research, whatever that was, instead of being a university or school teacher, as she and Terry had hoped he would be. She knew that she was wrong to feel disappointed; her children's lives were their own, and neither Terry nor she had ever wanted their children's careers caste in the same mould as theirs had been. Anyway, she knew perfectly well that the children had always been so much under the spell of their father that he had seemed the centre of their lives—she had been just one of the circle round him, as if she had been an elder sister rather than a mother. That had never worried her; and so she could understand, without resentment, why it was that now Terry was dead, she and the children seemed less closely bound together, seemed even less to share the same purpose. It was wrong, she thought, for parents to need their children's lives to give themselves purpose—how often Terry used to say that. You had to let them make their own lives, just as you went on making your own, up to the day you died.

So, she isolated herself, even to the extent of never going to Verderdorp, even on her days off duty. She couldn't really afford the luxury of a car, and anyway, she didn't like the thought of driving on her own; although once she drove there with Dr. Redman, by the time she got home she was so flustered with the heat and the swirling dust of the journey that next time he offered her a lift she refused. She had everything she needed already, she said; and what little she did in fact need she asked Caroline to buy and post to her.

The Superintendent hardly ever appeared, except for meals and to make a daily tour of the settlement; he didn't even come to the Sunday service since he was a member of the Reformed Church and spent most of Sunday in Verderdorp, at his church and visiting friends. Mrs. Allen knew that there was nothing that could be done about the Superintendent; if he had been a Church appointee, she would have written to the Bishop to tell him of the man's total incompetence and lack of concern. The Superintendent had the power of the law behind him; she had only the power of work—and provided he left her to work as she saw fit she would simply ignore him. At meal times she chatted politely to Dr. Redman and said not a word to Mr. Schwartz; that, and the hours she worked every day, was her only demonstration against him. What more could you expect from a man like that but a lack of concern, she thought.

But Dr. Redman disappointed her—he should have been an ally but somehow he wasn't. Oh, he did his job well enough; the concern for the ill and the injured was remarkable—his diagnoses were scrupulous and his remedies, as far as she could tell, sensible. He welcomed her re-organization of the nursing staff; he complimented her on getting the rubbish dump moved; he thanked her for improving the standard of staff meals; he helped her in setting up the créche; he admired her rockery; but somehow his thanks and compliments were cynical. Similarly, when she brought her blistered hands to him for treatment after her venture at hoeing, he roared with laughter and, it seemed to her, almost deliberately hurt her in painting the raw patches with iodine. And there was still that other thing about him, the way he had spoken about Dr. Allen, the way he spoke to the two younger nurses, the way he looked at the prettier African women who came to him for treatment, the way he appeared almost to fondle the young girls whom he treated for burns and cuts and sores. But she put that out of her mind; that was unthinkable.

Mrs. Allen made two more attempts to become friends with Simbele. First, after she had been three days in the settlement, she went one morning across the dust-bowl to the school. She knocked at the door of the classroom and, when Simbele appeared, asked him if it was a convenient time for her to visit. He bowed and moved aside for her to enter. As she came in, all the children, from the eight- to the fifteen-year-olds, stopped working, put their pens and pencils down, shut their books, and sat straight upright in their desks, all with their arms crossed carefully. "Do tell them to go on with whatever they were doing," she said to Simbele; and he spoke to them in Sotho, but they did not appear to understand him, for though one or two of the children opened their books again, when they saw that their class-mates still sat rigid, they shut them again and resumed their careful watching. "Please tell them to go on, Mr. Simbele," she said again; "I want simply to watch, I don't want to inspect them."

"They are not used to visitors, ma'am," said Simbele. "I do not think that they will work while you are here." So, helplessly, Mrs. Allen was forced to leave almost immediately; once she was outside the room, she peered cautiously through one of the windows and saw that the children had started work again and that Simbele was in front of the class, writing something on the board. Of course, she thought, when he spoke to them in Sotho, he did not really try to persuade them to go on with their work; and for a moment she felt anger against this man, who would not allow her to be herself, but who insisted on suspecting her—but then she forced herself to remember the injustices that were done to educated Africans like Simbele every moment of every day, and she tried to forgive him.

A week later she wrote a note to Simbele and invited him to tea with her that afternoon. She sent the note over with one of the nurses; and he came. But he refused to sit down, refused her offer of tea and the cake that she had made specially for the occasion, and refused to say anything, except to answer, politely but without any warmth at all, the questions she asked him.

After that Mrs. Allen stopped trying; Simbele, she realized, was determined to keep her at a distance—and if he was not prepared to accept her gestures of friendliness, why then, she thought, I can only hope that I shall persuade him not to hate me by the example I set in being prepared to accept other people only for what they themselves are, and in being prepared to work as hard as I can for the under-privileged. Work, that was what would persuade people like Simbele to accept her. Living meant working; loving people meant working for them. So, knowing that she was working for them, she found a kind of peace in herself, for the first time since Terry had died.

Yet she was not entirely happy. Partly the sense of trouble came from inside herself—it was revealed both in her dreams and in the inadequacy of the ritual she practised to free herself from the dreams. Certainly the dreams were terrible—dreams of perpetual fire and choking dust, of storms that blew the roofs from houses, hurled down trees and toppled mountains, of armed men and mutilated corpses, of circles of immobile stone through which she would wander lost and afraid, of stones which were suddenly alive and which clawed at her, of leering faces and of voices that spoke from the empty air; and certainly her closed-eyed whispering of the dreams to the dead husband did not entirely free her from the dreams, for they came back again and again, night after night. Partly the sense of trouble came from her relationships with the other people on the settlement; from her realization that the Superintendent, after all the successor of the Allen tradition, whether he liked it or not, was a useless man, incompetent and unconcerned; from her inability to trust or even to like Dr. Redman; from her failure to make any kind of sense with Simbele—she wanted so much to be friends with him, she wanted him to understand how much she respected the work he did for his people, she wanted the children to like her and she wanted to know them as she had known the children at Terry's school. She wasn't lonely; she had the company of her memory and the company of the past, and she was on ancestral ground—that made her strong, she thought; but she wanted to understand the people she worked with, she wanted to like them and them to like her.

But perhaps most important of all, she realized, the sense of trouble existed outside herself, had existed before she came, would exist even if she had not come. She was not sure what it was but it revealed itself in the way people watched each other so carefully, in the sullen formality with which they treated their overlords, in the way they would break off conversation when strangers approached, in the way they came out of their huts to watch, stonily, the police on their routine visits to the settlement. Yet it was so difficult to be sure about—where did it come from, she would wonder. Oh, there were causes enough, she knew: poverty, ignorance, dirt; but those had always existed and she had known them before, she had seen them in the townships near Terry's school, she and Terry had worked to eradicate them; but there had been a cheerfulness, a gaiety there, and here there was only sullenness and defeat.

Perhaps it was the air of defeat, thought Mrs. Allen, that was at the heart of this feeling, this hatred: no, not hatred, she corrected herself, unless hatred could be apathetic—it was a sort of dull ache, like a wound that had healed but had left the muscles tortured under the skin, or a slow poison, over the years, the poison of dust and red rock and the eroding winds.

Yet always she was borne up by her certainty that she was doing work that would please her dead husband, since it would create love. The routine of work was vital—she could live with her dreams, she was prepared to live with them, she would force herself to live with them, without concealing them from herself, without covering up their meaning even to herself. Living meant working; loving meant working; so, in her isolation, she worked even harder, and found inside herself a tired peace. More than that she could not feel.

She allowed herself only one luxury; and although she called it that to herself, no one would have guessed that it was a luxury, since all it was was her daily visit to the cemetery. Usually she went early in the morning before breakfast, before many people were about; she would walk slowly through the graves until she was drawn, almost involuntarily, to Dr. Allen's grave; and then she would stand there, motionless, sometimes for as long as twenty minutes, in a state of half-prayer and half-trance. She even grew used to old Joseph, who would most mornings appear from his hut when she arrived and who would cackle his high-pitched laugh and who would walk slowly over to where she stood looking at the grave and who would lay his daily flowers on the grave as she stood watching and who would then return to his digging of a slowly deepening grave; and while he scratched at the ground, Mrs. Allen would stand at the grave which she had taken almost for her own particular property and would dream of the past and of her dead husband. It wasn't that he was only with her then, when she was at the grave-side: he was always with her, he would always be with her—but when she was there, at the grave, she allowed herself to think of him. If grief was a vulture hovering over her, waiting to overwhelm her, he was the sun itself.

PART TWO

Voices in an empty house

VI

The trouble came in a way which only a few people in the region had expected.

Of course, there had been trouble before—indeed, the settlement had been founded in troubled times, for the tribesmen had always resented the loss of their traditional herding grounds to the white settlers. After Dr. Allen had been there only five years, the tribesmen to the north had risen up against the settlers, had murdered a hated tax-collector and his black servants, and had ambushed a commando of white farmers bent on punishment. Then they had tried their strength against a punitive expedition of the white settlers and had been outmanœuvred and slaughtered; Mrs. Allen knew all about that, for it was at that time that Dr. Allen had first established his reputation outside the valley. A party of the fleeing Tswana tribesmen had taken refuge in the settlement from a commando of whites bent on revenge; the commando had halted just outside the settlement, which in those days was fortified, and had sent in a message demanding that the tribesmen be surrendered. Dr. Allen had gone out, unarmed, and had argued for the tribesmen's lives; when he had not been able to persuade the settlers that the slaughter had already gone too far, he managed to persuade them that they should put up their strongest fighter to do battle alone with him, the winner to have possession of the fugitives. Of course he had won; and, of course, the settlers had cheered him and had ridden off.

Then there had been the trouble, at the turn of the century, in St. Joseph's itself. The people of the settlement had, for some reason that was never completely clear, but that was supposed to have something to do with food distribution, banded together and had attacked the white staff of the settlement; they had killed eight of the ten whites then on the settlement, women and children as well as the men; the two who survived were both children who were spirited away and hidden by their black nannies.

Then in the nineteen-twenties there had been a serious riot; but the whites managed to summon the police that time, and no whites were killed although the police shot the African ringleaders after calling them to a parley; and, five years before, a party of convicts working for one of the local farmers had escaped, had murdered the white farmer, his wife, and the three overseers, and had then been trapped in the mountains by a party of pursuing policemen, whom they held off for two days before surrendering. But recently the region had been very quiet; political trouble was, for most of the local people, white and black, something that happened in other places.

So it was even more surprising and, for some, terrifying, when unexpectedly, a band of apparently not local terrorists attacked, late one night, a farm lying twelve miles the other side of the mountains to the south-east of the settlement; the farmer who, foolishly, ran out into the yard when the attack started, firing wildly at the outhouses from which the terrorists had opened fire, was killed immediately, but the farmer's wife managed to get a call through to the local police before the terrorists got into the house. But what was most serious about this attack was that when the two police land-rovers from Grysberg came through the narrow defile on the main road just before the turning to the farm, they were ambushed by a larger and better-armed group of terrorists, who had blocked the road with rocks and bushes; although the police managed to get a radio call to their local headquarters, they did not stand a chance, for the terrorists were armed with what appeared to be modern automatic rifles and sub-machine guns. All twelve of the policemen, four white and eight black, were killed; all the arms they carried were captured; and their land-rovers were set on fire and destroyed. Only one of the terrorists was killed; before they left, the terrorists must have poured petrol over him and set his body alight, presumably so that he could in no circumstance be identified. By the time the Grysberg police managed to get reinforcements from Verderdorp, it was too late to catch the terrorists; by the time they got dogs there the scent had vanished; and even the spotter planes and the helicopters sent next day by the army failed to find any trace of them in the mountains around. Indeed, so effectively did they disappear that it was generally supposed that the band had moved a good distance away, perhaps even back over the border into the neighbouring African state of Botswana, from which it was supposed that they had come.

VII

Strangely enough, although the attack had taken place less than twenty miles away, there was not much reaction apparent in the settlement; each valley seemed very separate from the next, if only because of the mountains, which, if they were not high, were still difficult terrain, thickly covered with thorn-bush and unsteady boulders, and deeply ravined. The black people had learned to be careful and, whatever they may have felt, showed no feeling either way. Dr. Redman treated the whole business with something like hilarity, as if the policemen thoroughly deserved what they had got, and as if the police and their military reinforcements were necessarily too stupid to catch the fugitives; and Mrs. Allen, though she found Redman's attitude callous and silly, had already deliberately cut herself off from almost everything except the settlement, and so found it difficult to connect consciously the attack on the farmer and on the police with anything that happened in the settlement. Of the white people, the only person who reacted publicly was the Superintendent; and his reaction was so ludicrous to everyone except himself that it too did not seem to be connected.

For, as soon as news of the attack reached the settlement, Mr. Schwartz disappeared into Verderdorp and came back, a few hours later, with a Colt revolver which he wore strapped to his side like any cowboy in a Western. He took to wearing this whenever he appeared from his quarters and, for a few mornings at least, and immediately after his daily tour of the settlement, went off to a convenient hillside and could be heard practising firing the revolver. But even this seemed to make no difference to the black people on the settlement; they treated him just as they had always treated him, with a kind of superficial humility that concealed perfect indifference. In fact, the only person the Superintendent had to threaten with the revolver was Redman; and even that was not much of a threat.

Redman had heard from his patients that the Superintendent had been seen that morning wearing the revolver; and he had heard the Superintendent practising outside the settlement; so, at dinner that evening, when the Superintendent entered the staff dining-room, he leapt to his feet, clicked his heels, threw up a Nazi salute, and cried out, "Heil Herr Diktator". The Superintendent stared fixedly at Redman for a moment or two, and then, almost casually, dropped his hand to the butt of the revolver. Mrs. Allen thought, for a moment, that Redman was actually afraid, for he seemed to hesitate and then subside. But the moment the Superintendent sat down, Redman started again; turning to Mrs. Allen, he drawled out, "Say, ma'am, have you heard that we have a new marshal in town? The deadly Six-Shooter Schwartz, terror of tin-cans and stray butterflies. Don't you cross his path, ma'am, because he is mean and ugly." He put such emphasis on the last word that Mrs. Allen thought the Superintendent must act. But he did not, seemed rather to have made up his mind that reaction was useless; and although Redman tried again, a little later, to tease some reaction out of him, he failed again.

Mrs. Allen knew that the Superintendent was silly and frightened; but she knew too that she was not on Redman's side. Rather, she felt a vague pity for Mr. Schwartz; and anyway she was growing increasingly wary of Redman. There was something monstrous about him, something underhand, something almost dirty. Without meaning to, she had found herself watching him, watching his behaviour with the patients, his attitude to the nurses; and once she had walked through one of the wards into the nurses' duty room and had interrupted what she took to be an indecent approach by Dr. Redman to one of the nurses—and, although she had tried hard to put an innocent construction on it, that was what it had looked like, for the nurse had been terribly flustered by her arrival and Dr. Redman had been more than usually brazen. If her interpretation of the situation was right, she thought, she felt sorry for the nurse involved; how difficult it must be for her, having to fend off advances from a man she had to work for. So now, when the Superintendent left the dining-room, and when Redman turned to her to say, for once seriously, "Don't you think that his behaviour is almost insane, Mrs. Allen? I mean, I know I made a joke about it, but don't you think we should warn the Bishop, *your* bishop I should say, that the man is likely to go berserk at any moment and start slaughtering us and the Africans?" she answered, as coldly as she was capable of, "That is most disloyal of you, Dr. Redman; and though I do not think I approve of the Superintendent wearing a gun like that, I do not think we should criticize him behind his back."

Dr. Redman roared with forced laughter, and leaned across the table to her to say, "You're quite right, of course; it would not be sporting of us, would it? It wouldn't be behaviour befitting of ladies and gentlemen, a lady and a not quite gentleman at least." Then he sat back in his chair and, looking straight at her, said, "Really Mrs. Allen, you are the most stupid woman I have ever met."

* * *

She had another of the terrible dreams that night. She was standing on a high bank above a very long and wide road and coming down the road towards her was a motor-car in which there was someone whom she knew but whose name she could not think of. Suddenly on the bank opposite her there appeared a crowd of screaming, gesticulating men, each one armed with a gun as the Superintendent had been; and as the car sped down the road towards them, they tipped down the bank barrel after barrel of petrol, and, as each barrel burst, they threw lighted sticks down so that there was a barrier of flame across the road. Then she knew that Terry was in the car and she was trying to make him stop the car in time; and, on the high bank, she was trying to scream and couldn't and she was waving her arms above her head but they were so heavy that she could not lift them; and the car crashed into the flame, and through it, and turned over crazily and smashed into the bank below her, throwing the driver on to the road. And somehow she was down on the road, and the people and the car and the fire had disappeared, and she was walking slowly towards Terry's body; and as she walked, she could see that he was still alive, because his hands were moving; but she couldn't walk faster; and just as she got to the body, it sat upright, and it wasn't Terry at all, but was Simbele, and he opened his mouth and laughed, just as Redman had laughed, and leaned forward and was about to speak when a great stream of blood burst from his mouth. And she was in a crowd of strangers and she was looking for someone and they knew where he was but every time she asked one of them for help in finding him, he turned his back; and then the crowd began to press closer and closer to her, so that she could not force her way through, could not move at all, could not breathe, and she began to strike them, and to curse obscenely, and to weep.

She forced herself out of the dream then and back to wakefulness; but when she woke she was still dreaming, and she did not realize, and there was something wrong with her, and she was lying on the operating table in the new surgery and Dr. Redman, in his white surgeon's coat, and surrounded by the nurses also in white surgical clothes, was coming towards her and instead of a scalpel he carried in his hand some obscene thing which he wanted to thrust into her mouth and she was screaming again because she knew that she had already woken up and that this couldn't be a dream. And that was gone and she was in the cemetery and was walking towards old Joseph, who was digging a grave and as she got to him he turned round and he had Terry's face and he was smiling at her; and suddenly she was weeping in enormous gasps and gulps and the noise of her own weeping wakened her. And that was not much relief, for though she tried to whisper it aloud as she would have done when Terry as alive, she carried the horror of her dream with her for the next two days—it was only the horror of actuality that made it submerge again.

Two days after her dream she confirmed all her worst suspicions about Dr. Redman, for although it seemed to happen entirely by chance, perhaps she wanted it to happen.

Usually, after lunch, Mrs. Allen, like most people on the settlement, rested for an hour or two, for the heat made it impossible to work effectively. But this afternoon, with the memory of the dream still strong upon her, she found it impossible even to lie resting on her bed; she tried an arm-chair instead, but that too seemed almost dangerous—what if she fell asleep and that dream came back? So, eventually, she abandoned rest and went to see that everything in the hospital wards was decently tidy and clean. She found Sister Mbele in the nurses' duty room, alone, half-asleep in the single arm-chair, with her feet on the table, and her white skirt indecently rucked up over her fat thighs; as Mrs. Allen came in, Sister Mbele hurriedly took her feet off the table, pulled her skirt down, and stood up.

"Sorry to disturb you, Sister," Mrs. Allen said. "I thought that I would look round the wards to see that everything was all right," and when Sister Mbele made a movement as if to accompany her, "No, don't you worry to come. I shall go by myself—you go on with your rest."

Everything was, as she knew it would be, perfectly in order;

the four men in the men's ward were lying quietly, either asleep or seeming to be; Mrs. Allen noted that they all seemed comfortable and then opened the linen wardrobes at the end of the room just to see that everything there was tidy too. It was; and Sister Mbele deserves a compliment, thought Mrs. Allen, for the manner in which she keeps this place—really, she is a thoroughly competent soul, always willing, always spotlessly clean. She went through to the women's ward, noting as she did so that it was time for the walls of the short corridor to be painted again; she must remember, she thought, to mention this to the Superintendent. Everything in the women's ward was equally clean and tidy; she stopped to say a word to old Mrs. Doleni, who had come into the hospital two weeks earlier after a fall outside her daughter's hut—looking at her, Mrs. Allen knew that she would die soon; her skin looked almost more grey than black and her eyes were as vacant as those of a very young baby—she doesn't seem to know even that I am talking to her, thought Mrs. Allen; well, perhaps it is better that way. She moved on past a few empty beds to talk to the two younger African women, who had been in only a day or two to have their babies; one was asleep and the other so drowsy that Mrs. Allen did not bother to stop but went straight over to the glass partition at the end of the ward, behind which was the small nursery. The two babies lay in cots and Mrs. Allen had to stretch to see them; they too were both asleep, great fat black babies wrapped in the white and blue blankets of the hospital. Suddenly she looked again; one was asleep, yes, but the other ... asleep? Or was she seeing something else? For the baby seemed somehow to be shaking, as if it were in a spasm. Frantically, Mrs. Allen threw open the door of the nursery and bent down over the cot; yes, the baby was in spasm—and she could hear its hurried, irregular, urgent breathing, almost as if ... as if ...

Mrs. Allen did not run down the ward; she did not want to

frighten the mothers, especially as she wasn't sure which one the sick baby belonged to; but she moved as quickly as she could and, once she was in the corridor, ran; she burst into the nurses' duty room, had to shake Sister Mbele to wake her, and shouted, "Go to get Dr. Redman. One of the babies is very sick," and when the sister didn't seem to understand her, she shouted, "Wake up, damn you. Get the doctor. Run, you fool, There's a baby sick." She turned away then to go back to see if there was anything she could do while the woman ran the hundred yards to the Doctor's cottage; but, to her amazement, when she was half-way down the ward again, she realized that the sister had not gone, but was immediately behind her.

"I told you to get the doctor. Do you hear me?" she screamed now, "Get the doctor." But the sister stood there, not moving, not moving even when Mrs. Allen shook her by the shoulders, in an attempt to make her understand. And then she shook her head. "No," she said, "No."

"What do you mean? No? No? Get the doctor, I said," shouted Mrs. Allen, not caring now about disturbing the others in the ward. The sister still did not obey and, in utter exasperation and rage, Mrs. Allen shook her again and went herself.

Outside, the slight wind of the afternoon was thrusting and jerking the dust between the buildings, and the fine dust in the air seemed to make the sun even more glaring than usual. As she ran, stumbling in the shallow depressions, Mrs. Allen noted, with that small part of her conscious mind that was not concerned with the sick baby, that the clouds over to the west were gathering together into storm shapes, almost like the raised fist of a man, monstrously reflected in the sky; there would be a storm before evening, though the chances were that there would either be no rain, just the usual summer storm of thunder in the distance, or so much so quickly that it would not help the farmers. She must hurry, she thought.

She saw, as she came up to Dr. Redman's house, that all the curtains were drawn; he was probably asleep, she thought, for he seemed to have a young man's almost infinite capacity for sleep—he was nearly always late for breakfast and sometimes did not appear at all until Mrs. Allen sent one of the nurses to wake him. She raised her hand to bang on his door but then, for some reason that afterwards she could not explain to herself, though she thought that perhaps unconsciously she must have heard something, she did not knock but went instead to the window. She could see nothing through the front window; the curtains were too securely drawn. So she went to the back where, by bending down, she could just see; it seemed very dark inside the bedroom but after a second or two she could see —and what she saw made her start, stand up quickly, and begin to turn away in horror. But as she turned, she hesitated, looked around to see if there was anyone in sight who could see her at the window, and then bent to look again.

No, there was no mistake about it. There was Nurse Peters, and she was naked, and she was lying right on the end of Dr. Redman's divan, and her legs were spread wide, and, also naked, and kneeling on the ground, between her legs, and thrusting in at her body, was Dr. Redman. As Mrs. Allen watched, fascinated and horrified, Dr. Redman suddenly thrust himself away from the woman's body and stood up; and Nurse Peters laughed, and sat up, and leaned forward so that she could reach round Redman's back, and she pulled his body close to her and she began to caress him with her mouth, while his body shook convulsively and his hands grabbed and tore at her tightly curling black hair.

Mrs. Allen managed to get three or four steps away from the window before she vomited; in one part of her mind she could hear, whispering and pleading, her own voice, crying No No No to the dark places of her mind, where there was another voice, saying something that she could not and would not hear.

And the voices were growing louder and louder, and there were more and more of them, and they were screaming and yelling inside her head, and she had to bring her hand up to her mouth to press the voices back so that they could not say in public what they said in her mind. She turned then, and with the back of her hand still pressed to her mouth so that she could feel her teeth bruising her lips, she began to stumble back towards the hospital.

But as she walked, her conscious mind began to take control again; the whole business began to take shape in her mind now —she had been right to suspect Dr. Redman, her intuition about his uncontrolled sensuality had been right; and that Nurse Peters, with her friendliness and charm and rich black prettiness, why, she was a disgusting hypocrite, pretending purity when all the time she was doing that with Dr. Redman; and perhaps she had heard something at the door of Redman's cottage which made her not knock but go instead to the window. Yes, the pieces were all there now, everything was clear. Mrs. Allen forced herself to admit even charity to her disgust; it was just possible that Redman and Nurse Peters were in love and wanted to marry, she said to herself, forcing herself to be sensible even in this situation—for she was not a prude. She had loved her husband passionately, with her mind and her body, and she knew that between lovers nothing was dirty; but even as she said it to herself, even as she remembered all that had happened between Terry and herself, she knew that she did not believe that those two were in love. She would have noticed before, and she would have known it by the way they treated each other's bodies; there had been something so controlled about Dr. Redman's carefully timed withdrawal, something lewd about Nurse Peters's laugh as she had started to do that thing to him, something disrespectful about everything that had happened between them. No, she did not believe that there was anything like love between them; what she had seen disgusted her, and there was no love in it, there was only sensuality.

Suddenly she stopped. She had remembered the sick baby. She had to get Dr. Redman, she thought; no matter what was happening in there, she had to get him. Whatever he was in himself, he was a doctor; and that child needed him, no matter how disgusting he was. She must put that thing out of her mind.

When she knocked at the door of Dr. Redman's house, a few moments later, she heard, almost as if it had been someone else who was hearing so remote did it seem to her, the sound of whispering, and then a scurry. She didn't look at Dr. Redman when he came to the door but she saw behind him that the door of the bedroom was shut.

"What's the trouble, Mrs. Allen?" he asked.

Still without looking at him, she said, "There's one of the babies which seems to be ill—it's in some kind of spasm. I think you had better come."

Immediately, he was the professional again. "I'll be about two minutes. I must put on shoes and wash," and then he added, lamely it seemed to her, "I've been asleep." No, thought Mrs. Allen, although you don't know that I know, you haven't, you liar; and, as he opened the bedroom door, she looked up from the dust where she had fixed her eyes while she spoke to him, and she saw that he had had time, before he answered her knock at the door, to slip on a pair of slacks and a shirt, although his feet were still bare. But there was no sign of Nurse Peters for the brief moment that the bedroom door was open. But she was there, she knew; and if she went round to the back of the house while Dr. Redman went to the hospital, and waited there quietly for a few minutes, she would, she knew, catch Nurse Peters when she left. That would be definite proof, if she needed anything more than what she had already seen; and she would be able to say to Nurse Peters what was in her mind now. But there was no need to do that; she had seen everything already; and, without waiting for Dr. Redman to re-emerge, she turned to walk back to the hospital.

After she had walked a few slow yards, Dr. Redman passed her, running. As he passed, he turned his head to her and shouted, "Is Sister Mbele there?"

"Yes," she called back; and stopped suddenly. Of course, she thought, that was it; that was why Sister Mbele had refused to call him. She had probably known what was happening there—and she had been shaken by the shoulders and had been called a fool. Poor woman! She must remember to apologize to her, though she wouldn't be able to explain that she understood now. She would have to say that she had been overwrought by finding the baby in spasm; and she would have to leave the Sister to assume that she had not discovered what had been happening in the doctor's bedroom.

Standing in the middle of the dusty bowl of the settlement, Mrs. Allen was hardly conscious of the heat, of the fine dust settling around her feet and on her shoes, of old Joseph's far-away and high-pitched chanting as he worked in the cemetery up the hillside, of the shouts of the children playing behind the huts, of the monotonous clank clank clank of the water pump; "How terrible!" she said aloud. How terrible! and she would have to do something about it. She could not allow such a thing to go on. O Terry, Terry, said a voice in her mind, what shall I do now? You would know what to do. Then another voice said, It's simple really: go and tell the Superintendent, and he will tell the police, and the police will come, and Dr. Redman and Nurse Peters will go to gaol, for they are breaking the law, a white man and a black woman doing that kind of thing together. But another voice said, No, Terry would not approve, nor you yourself; neither of you believed that immorality was a matter for the State—besides, if you did something like telling the police, you would simply be avoiding your own responsibility to do something to stop that terrible thing, that lack of love using the gestures of love. No, she would have to keep this to herself, she would have to do what had to be done on her own. Again she said, again aloud, "How terrible!"

VIII

Rubbing a hand wearily across his forehead, Simbele turned from the blackboard on which he had been explaining, without much conviction he knew, the causes of the first Anglo-Boer war to the small group of senior pupils sitting attentively on the right side of the classroom; although he had run ten minutes over the usual time for the end of afternoon school, he could see that only one of his sixty pupils showed any sign of impatience—and he, Simbele knew, was making half a crown a week looking after the small son of one of the white farmers farther up the valley and was worried that he should not be late—so Simbele nodded to him and said, "Michael, you may go if you wish," and quickly the boy slipped out of his desk and ran. Then he spoke louder so that everyone could hear: "It is time to go now; finish what you are doing and then go." Some of the smaller children at the back, who had been making careful little drawings of the settlement in chalk on their slates, began to chatter quietly and to show each other what they had done, so that one of the senior pupils, Mary Shungu, concentrating on copying down what her teacher had written on the board, turned to whisper, "Shh!"; gradually, as each child finished what he had done and collected his books together, the classroom emptied. As he waited, Simbele watched the senior pupils copying down his own carefully written version of what he had spent the afternoon explaining; he wondered if his lack of conviction about the importance of it communicated itself to the pupils—it was so terribly difficult to tell what they really felt; you could tell with the little ones, but these . . . they had learnt to sit still and to learn what he told them as best they could. There was never any problem about making them learn; they knew that what he told them, what the syllabus laid down by the Department of Bantu Education forced him to tell them, was, for whatever limitations they could in fact see in it, still their only chance to escape; or that was what they thought, anyway, for they did not know, and would not believe him if he told them, that it was only escape to another kind of prison, perhaps an even smaller one than the settlement and the mines and the white houses and the fields. The hardest thing to do was to make them ask questions, to ask, "What were our people doing while the white tribes were at war?" The syllabus didn't expect them to ask that question; and the few books they had access to didn't ask that question; and even if they asked him, he would be able to reply only in terms of folk-lore, imagination and guess-work, and what they wanted was to know How many? When? How? And who would blame them, he thought. Sometimes he would try to explain, and would forget to talk in English, and he would tell them what he thought must have happened, and they would listen, and they wouldn't write anything down, and he would have stopped them if they had tried to, in case some traitor was there to give a record of what he said to the police—but they still did not ask questions, they listened as if in terror that they should miss anything, but they had been brought up not to ask questions, especially those which could not be answered.

They were all finished now, except for Petrus Mbele, who was the slowest of them but who made up for it by fanatically hard work; and presently the classroom was empty except for Simbele and the boy, and then he too finished, put his pencil and books away, and walked slowly up to Simbele's table. He stopped in front of the table, fished in the pocket of his shirt, and brought out a carefully folded square of paper, which he placed on the desk in front of his teacher. He waited until Simbele had opened the paper, then turned and left.

So he's the one, thought Simbele; they had told him that was how they would do it when the time came. He had expected it to be one of the little ones; but they had, he thought, chosen well in Petrus—he was slow but he was meticulous. He wouldn't make mistakes, he wouldn't boast to the other children, he would not talk even to his mother, he would not be excited; but he would know what had to be done and he would do it slowly and deliberately.

Simbele looked at the note; it was written in pencil, carefully, in capital letters, and it said only, "Tonight urgently. At the mouth of the Narrow Tooth Gorge. As usual otherwise." He went over to look at one of the large-scale ordnance maps which he had pinned on the wall of the classroom. The place was further away, perhaps half an hour more walking, and he might have to leave a little earlier than before; but he knew the way—at least as far as Van Breda's farm—and he would be able to find it, even in the darkness. He had better take the rest of the food, although last time they had told him that they had enough and that he need not bring it; of course, the fact that Petrus had brought him the message meant that they were in touch with other people in the valley—they probably got food from them. I wonder why they want me again, he thought; it was strange, but perhaps it was only that they needed to see other people sometimes—it must be difficult for them there in the mountains, when they had to be so careful to move only when they could not be seen. He had been worried when the planes had come; they had seemed to move so slowly over the mountains, hovering, checking, repeating a pattern suddenly, from side to side and up and down, like vultures; and he had heard that there were still some soldiers in the mountains, searching, in case they hadn't gone back over the border. There would be more risk now in going to them; but they had risked more—and they would, he knew, eventually, lose more.

Of course, they had prepared everything very carefully. They had trained for years somewhere up in the north; and they had sent Moshi back six months before they had come themselves, and he had found out everything that they needed to know; and they had all been there in the mountains for a full month before everything had happened—this wasn't a suicide squad, he knew, this was a military group; they would probably die but they had not come back for death only—at least not for their own deaths.

Sitting at his table, with his hands over his eyes to shut out the bright glare of the afternoon sun coming in through the windows, Simbele remembered; he hadn't meant to get involved again—that had been all over even before he came out of prison. That had been all over after the two months the warders had kept him in a cell just below the row of cells where they kept the men to be executed. That was one of the few things that he had not been able to forget; why, if he listened, he could still hear the singing of the men waiting to die as clearly as if they had been singing outside the classroom. The warders used to tell them only three days before exactly when they were to be hanged—usually when the news of the failure of their appeals came through to the Governor; they had known then that there would be no reprieve, they had known then exactly when it was that they would be taken down that long passage, through the little door, to the thin ropes round their hands, to the bandages round their eyes, to the thick ropes round their necks, to the little platform where they would stand forever. At first they would scream and shout for mercy and forgiveness— but there was none, and so all they had left was to sing, sing every freedom song until they forgot freedom, sing the drinking songs and the bawdy songs, and then sing the hymns, until they could do nothing more than whisper the words and the music to their own ears. But right below them you could hear even the whispers; and you would lie awake those last nights just as they lay awake. Sometimes they hanged as many as six men together on the same morning; and you would hear their whispered singing all through the night; and you would hear the warders coming in the early morning, and the priest, and the men would still sing, would sing all the way down that passage, until the little door closed their voices away; and you waited until you knew that it must be over. But for you it wasn't over, because in that place they executed men twice a week.

When he had come out, his brother, the businessman of the family, had offered to pay for him to leave the country and go to some other country where the fact that he had been in gaol for his politics would make him welcome; but he had refused that. He hadn't wanted to get involved again, but he hadn't wanted to leave. He had wanted to be a teacher again; and he couldn't be, because he had his name and that name was now a bad one. So he had borrowed twenty pounds from his brother, and with fifteen pounds of it he had bought a new identity—or that was part of it, at least, because he had bought a new pass book from the crooked clerk at the Bantu Administration offices in Newlands and he had taken the name of Johannes Simbele, who came from Tswanaland, who was three years younger than he was, and who was a teacher; he had left Johannesburg without telling even his brother, and he had walked, avoiding the big towns, for two months, eating when he could, sleeping in the huts of hospitable tribesmen or in the fields. When he had started that walk he had been a big man, almost fat, because although he had worked hard in prison he had eaten regularly; by the time he reached Tswanaland he was a thin man and, when he looked at his face in a mirror, he saw only Johannes Simbele, aged thirty-eight, who had been born in these parts but who had been in Johannesburg for thirty-five years, which accounted for his unfamiliarity with the tribal dialect which the people of the region spoke; he even made enquiries in Verderdorp about a grandmother who, he said, had once lived there. So he grew to be one person again, and kept out of police trouble, and carried his pass everywhere he went; and for three months he worked as houseboy for a white family in Verderdorp and then he heard that the settlement needed a teacher and he walked the twenty miles out there and the Superintendent was so relieved to have an application at all that he forgot to ask Simbele for testimonials; or perhaps he thought it wiser not to, for teachers were hard to come by in that region. He had been five years there now, and sometimes it seemed to him that he had been born only the moment he had walked out of that clerk's room with the name of Johannes Simbele instead of the one he had been known by, because it wasn't simply the names that had changed, it was everything, tribe, family history, parents, brothers, childhood, beliefs, creeds, opinions, everything, even the way he looked in a mirror. There were some things that couldn't be changed, some memories that you could never shut away, but you learned to keep those secret; and you waited, teaching what you were meant to teach, and only sometimes teaching the truth, and then you were careful and made sure that no one wrote down what you said; and you waited, not for anything to happen, because you were not involved enough in anything that could happen to wait for it; and waited, perhaps only for that day when you were an old man and could return to walk unrecognized through the streets of Johannesburg.

Then, one day six months before, he had walked out of his classroom and Moshi had been there, talking to two of his pupils, and for one terrifying moment he had become a dead person, the person who had last seen Moshi ten years before, the month before his arrest, at a meeting at which he had been chairman and Moshi one of the district organizers of the People's Organization. He had heard in gaol that Moshi had left the country when the others had been arrested; and now he was back here, dressed like a tramp, grey with the dust of travelling. He hesitated for only a moment, then walked past, saying as he did so in the formal language of strangers, "Good day, my brother." Moshi, who had looked up as he came out of the classroom, had looked at him, then away, and suddenly back again, frowning and puzzled, yet gave him back the same formal greeting; and Simbele had walked on, without looking back, to his hut, where he had sat waiting to see if the dead person still walked in Johannes Simbele's guise.

When Moshi came to his hut, half an hour later, Simbele could see that he was still not sure, for he spoke formally when he gave his name.

"Your pupils tell me that your name is Simbele," he said and Simbele bowed assent. Moshi frowned at him in puzzlement and then, suddenly, as if he was staking everything on one throw, grinned and said challengingly, "Hello, Zac." Simbele looked at him for a long time before he answered, "Hello, Moshi." But he still stayed Simbele, and the next time Moshi used the old name, he stopped him and said, "My name is Johannes Simbele; and I shall kill you if you use the name of that other person."

Strange, thought Simbele, as he looked down the empty length of his classroom, that I should have said that I would kill him; for Moshi had threatened him in the same way—"Mr. Simbele, if that is your name, let me tell you that if you are an informer I shall kill you"—and for another moment he had again become the dead person, the person Moshi called Zac; and he had said in his old voice, the voice of the leader, the voice of authority, "In saying that you have already said too much. I know that you are doing something that I could inform on. Since I am not an informer (and you have only my word for that) you have better tell me what you are doing here."

Moshi had told him then: he was the advance guard of a party of freedom-fighters (Simbele made the correction to "terrorists" in his own mind; he never allowed his pupils to use euphemisms and he was not going to allow himself to use them now, even for the sake of the dead Zac; there was nothing wrong with the word "terrorist", for that was their method, even though it was not their aim), who were at this moment waiting just over the border of Botswana a little to the west of them. They had been told to come to this area, close enough to the border for an escape to be possible, under-populated, mountainous, among a tribe which had a reputation for loathing their white overlords; and he had come to find out what he could before the party moved in. Almost without thinking, Simbele found himself helping Moshi; he allowed Moshi to recruit him as a link-man, and he agreed to meet the rest of the party on a Tuesday night three weeks ahead, at a place which Moshi pointed out to him through his bedroom window—if no one was there that night, he was to come again the week later, and again the week later. So he had become involved again, even though he was Simbele the teacher, not Zac the trade unionist.

Well, thought Simbele, they had not asked him to do much yet; first, for some tins of food, then for a map, and he had got both very easily. Perhaps tonight, he thought, they will have something more for me to do. He looked at the clock on the shelf; I must eat now, he thought, and then I must sleep for three hours, and then it will be time to begin. Even if you had forgotten why you were doing something, the thing itself remained to be done; that at least you were sure about.

* * *

It was a little after midnight when Simbele reached the mouth of the Narrow Tooth gorge; after he had left the road, a mile before Van Breda's farm, and had cut across their lands, he had fallen twice—since he was hampered by the heavy haversack he carried, he had fallen heavily and, the second time, had torn his left hand badly on a sharp stone. Now, waiting for whoever was meeting him to arrive, he lit a match to see how deep the wound was; he had felt the blood running down his fingers as he walked, but even so he was surprised to see how bad it was. He put the wound to his mouth and sucked it to get rid of any particles of dirt that had not been bled away, spat the blood out, and then wrapped his handkerchief tightly around his hand, clasping the end between his fingers to keep it secure.

As he was doing this, a dark shadow detached itself from the other shadows at the side of the gorge and came towards him. He waited; this was always a bad moment. When the man was a few yards away from Simbele, he stopped and said, not in Tswana but in the argot of the townships, "Hullo, comrade." Simbele replied in the same argot, in the voice of Zac: "Greetings, comrade." Now that the man was closer, he could see, in the faint light of the stars, that he carried a rifle. Then from behind him came another voice, "Greetings, comrade." This is something new, thought Simbele; they didn't worry with this rigmarole last time—they were being more careful now. If I hadn't been the man they expected, they would perhaps have killed me; and if I had been with a party of police, they could have opened fire and so warned the rest of the party to get away. It must, he thought, have been bad for them while the planes were searching.

The second man did not come with them when the first led him away up the rocky side of the gorge, then up its rim, and then farther round and up, and down again, and up, and then still farther up; Simbele put out of his mind, quite deliberately, the route—he did not want to know any more than he needed to; anyway, it was such a bad climb that he could not remember anything, except the effort of concentration on each foothold and each step. The man in front seemed to know his way like a leopard would but he went slowly for Simbele's sake, stopping after each section of the climb and occasionally whispering advice back to him: "Watch the next bit; there's some loose rock. . . . Here give me your hand and I will pull you up. . . . We go sideways along that ledge now."

After they had climbed for twenty minutes, the man stopped. "Rest for a moment," he told Simbele and squatted down, unhitching his rifle from his back and using its butt as a support. Simbele sat too; he was breathing so hard that he could hear nothing but the agonized working of his lungs. But after a moment or two he could control his breathing and he sat quiet, listening to the night, listening to what seemed at first like silence and to what, after a moment or two, became a succession of quiet noises, dogs barking across the valley, bushes rustling, night-animals whispering and stalking, and, somewhere far below the noises that you could positively hear, the almost unheard collapse of stones and mountains and earth. Then suddenly Simbele heard some noise that was foreign, some noise that made him reach out to grab his guide's arm. "What's that?" Simbele asked.

"What?"

"That noise. Can't you hear?"

They both listened in the silence; nothing, and then Simbele heard it again, a low agonized moaning somewhere near them, almost mechanical so regular it seemed, yet agonized in a way no machine could reproduce. "Listen," said Simbele still clutching his guide's upper arm. "Surely you hear it?" It was so clear, and it was close to them.

"That?" said the man. "That is all right. I have grown so used to it that I did not hear it."

"But what is it?" asked Simbele. "Is it someone hurt? Who is it?"

"They will tell you," his guide stood up then. "Are you ready?" he asked and then whistled three times, looking up the cliff face below which they had been resting. From above them came two whistles in reply and, a moment later, a clattering and slithering as something came down the rocks. The guide pulled Simbele over to the cliff and started to tie the rope under his arms, explaining as he did so, "The cliff is too steep for most to climb alone, especially at night; so they will help you with the rope. You must walk with your feet against the cliff," and in the faint starlight he demonstrated with his hands, "leaning back against the rope. They will pull slowly so that you can keep your feet firmly."

"Are you coming after me?" Simbele asked.

"No," said the man. "I will wait here to take you back down again." Yes, thought Simbele, and even if the police got past your friend below, and came near here, you would be able to lead them away from the place, and your other friends could escape. He did not like the thought of leaning back against that rope as he walked up the side of a cliff; but if it was not now it would be later, and if they wanted him to go up there he would go up there.

"I am ready," he said to the guide, who stretched up and gave the rope three sharp tugs; immediately Simbele felt the rope grow completely taut—he leaned back against its pressure and it held him up; and (like a fly, he thought) he began to walk up the side of the cliff.

Twice on the short journey he slipped; the first time he swung round completely and his haversack crashed into the cliff face—for a moment or two he hung there helplessly and then managed to find a ledge; with that to support him he could begin to walk again. A moment or two later he slipped again and this time he managed, instinctively, to use his hands to protect himself, thrusting at the cliff as it came crashing against him. As he reached up again to grasp the rope above him, he felt the blood from the re-opened cut in his left hand begin to run down his arm.

They helped him carefully over the top and helped him to

stand; he was surprised to find how shaken he felt and it was a moment or two before he looked to see where he was. There were three men with him, standing on a broad ledge beyond which lay a shallow cave; it was lighter here, but he couldn't see the rest of the party. The moaning he had heard below was louder now, coming from somewhere at the back of the shallow cave; he had lost the sound during his climb—he could hear now that there was someone in there who was hurt. Was that why he had been summoned, he wondered.

The men led him into the shallow cave and as he went he realized that in the first large cave there was another smaller cave, the entrance of which had been concealed with some heavy material and with branches and piles of stones. One of the men lifted aside the material and Simbele stooped and pushed through.

The cave inside was lit by a small hurricane lamp standing on a small square packing case, with markings on it in a language which he could not understand. With the light of the lamp bright in his eyes that had long grown accustomed to darkness he could see that there were ten or twelve men lying around the edges of the cave. Behind them, propped against the wall, were their rifles, not the long elegant guns that sportsmen use, but shorter, bulging, squat weapons. The moaning was louder now and he could hear that it came from behind another curtain made of the same heavy dark material used to divide the cave into two. Without waiting to be shown the way, he pushed through this and came into the small back section of the cave. As he went in, someone sitting on the floor shone a torch straight into his face.

"Hullo, Zac," came Moshi's voice from behind the torch.

"Simbele," he corrected automatically. "You are blinding me with that torch," and the torch went out abruptly, leaving him even more blind. "Is it you that is hurt, Moshi?" he asked, though he knew it couldn't be; the moaning was so regular, as monotonous as a water-pump, almost as if the person who moaned had forgotten why he had begun but who went on because it was the only thing to be done.

"No," Moshi replied, and then, explaining his answer, switched the torch on again and directed its beam to a man lying next to him. As Simbele watched, Moshi swung the torch to the man's head. Simbele closed his eyes and waited for the click that would mean that he could no longer see. When he heard it he opened his eyes again and looked into the darkness in front of him.

"How did it happen? Was it during the thing with the police?" he asked Moshi, but before he could answer someone else, carrying the hurricane lamp, pushed in through the curtain. Simbele turned round, he recognized the man though he did not know his name—he had deliberately refused to be introduced to any of the men when Moshi had first brought him to their earlier hiding-places; he believed that the less he knew, the better—and he was fairly sure that this was the leader of the group, for the other men had treated him with deference. He was a tall man, nearly as tall as Simbele himself, thick-shouldered and long-armed, with heavy features and flecks of grey in his closely cropped curling black hair.

"Have you seen him?" the man asked Simbele.

"Yes. It seems very bad. Did it happen in the first raid, or with the police?"

"No," said the leader laconically.

Moshi explained: "He was cleaning a rifle two days ago, and he must have made a mistake. It is the whole of his jaw that is gone." You don't need to tell me, thought Simbele; I've seen that already, in that second or two that the torchlight had been on the man's head—I could see that even with the bandages. "What are you going to do with him?" he asked.

As if to answer, the leader walked forward and lifted the lantern so that its light showed the moaning injured man again.

Simbele forced himself to look, to see how, below the nose where the mouth should be, there was nothing, nothing except bloodstained bandages, an obscene emptiness. He looked away from the injured man and fixed his eyes on the steady flame of the lantern.

"What are you going to do?" he asked again.

"We have been giving him morphine," the man answered. He walked round where Moshi was sitting, back against the wall, and fumbled in a haversack to produce a syringe. He held it up and said, "I have been giving him as little as I can. But I have only enough left for two more days; and that is all that we have for all of us." There was a rustle of the curtain behind Simbele and two more men crowded in but he did not turn to look at them.

"Is that why you sent for me?" he asked.

"Yes," the leader said. "You have a hospital at the Mission settlement. Can you not get some more of this," and he gestured with the syringe, "perhaps from one of the nurses?"

Before Simbele could think of an answer, Moshi spoke: "What is the point?" he asked. "You will simply give him morphine till he dies."

"Yes," said one of the men behind Simbele. "Yes. There is only one thing we can do," and the other man went on, as if he were speaking in the same voice, "It will be very quick and he will feel nothing."

"I didn't mean that," said Moshi, looking up from the floor. "You know that I didn't mean that."

"Yes," said one of the men behind Simbele, now pushing forward so that he stood in the centre of the cave. "We know what you mean. You want us to call an ambulance and a doctor, perhaps even the police. 'Please come, Mr. Policeman,'" he mimicked Moshi's weary voice savagely, "'we have an accident here.'"

"Wait," said the leader quietly. "Simbele, what do you think? Can you get more morphine?"

"I don't think so," he answered carefully. "I hear that all the medicine is kept locked in a cupboard in the hospital, in the room they call the dispensary." It sounded inadequate, so he explained: "There was some stealing, you see, before; and the new matron put locks on to the doors of all the cupboards."

Moshi looked up from the floor. "But won't one of the nurses get it for you?"

Simbele pondered for a moment before answering. "I don't think it safe to ask any of them," he said. "They would have to break the cupboard and the police might be called. No, it would not be possible."

"You see," said the man in the centre of the cave, looking not at Simbele or the leader but at Moshi. "There is nothing we can do, except . . ." he hesitated then for a moment, ". . . killing him."

At least, thought Simbele, you have the courage to use the right words; you say the word "killing", you do not say "putting out of misery" or anything like that. He looked at the man; in the faint light of the lamp, he could see that he had a long wide scar running from the corner of his left eye right down his cheek to the edge of his chin.

"No," said Moshi, still with his head bent forward so that it rested on his knees. "We cannot do that."

"We must do that," said the man with the scarred face, taking a step forward towards Moshi, who still did not move. "You were very brave before; it was you who poured the petrol over Ledoni, and you who put the match to it. Now all you say is 'no'. You are a coward, Mdelini." Moshi was on his feet almost before the name was out; he lunged forward at the man and would have caught him if the leader had not moved quickly between them. "Both of you be quiet," he said. "I shall decide what we do," and he gestured at the injured man.

Simbele, in the shadows near the curtain, made up his mind and said, quietly, "I can get a doctor, I think."

Moshi pushed frantically past the two men between him and Simbele and said, "Where from? Where can you get a doctor from?" Simbele looked at him carefully, then said, "I'm not sure—I said that I think I can get a doctor. But there's a doctor in the settlement, a Jew, who will come."

Moshi grabbed his arm; "You must get him, you must," he burst out, shaking Simbele's arm to emphasize what he said. "You must get the doctor."

"What can even a doctor do?" growled the man behind Simbele.

"Precisely. I tell you, this one's dead, as good as dead," said his friend.

"Wait," said the leader, turning to Simbele. "How do you know he will come?"

"I do not know; I think. He is a friend of the people." Or, thought Simbele, that is one way of putting it—he could be persuaded. No, dammit, tell the truth, to yourself at least, he thought—blackmailed: that was the word—oh, very subtly, but he could be blackmailed. Simbele knew about Nurse Peters; and she was not the only one he knew about—there had been others before her, others at the same time for all he knew, and he knew that it wouldn't be long before there was another pretty young black girl recruited to the nursing staff. As far as he knew, everyone in the settlement, except perhaps the white people, knew about Dr. Redman and the nurses. He hadn't talked about it, but people knew. At least, some of the children did. He'd discovered some of them giggling over a drawing of two people, one male and white, one female and black, and both with grotesquely exaggerated sexual organs. He'd destroyed the drawing, had told the children not to be silly; but he had been sure that the jokes would continue. In a way, it seemed a pity now that he had burnt the drawing: he could have offered it to the Jew simply for sale—his price would have been attention to that grotesquely moaning thing in the corner.

But if he couldn't do that now, he could still make him come.

To the four silent men who had heard his offer, and in a way to the fifth man who could not hear him, he said, "Shall I try to get the doctor?"

"You are sure that he is a friend of the people, this white man," said the leader. In a way, thought Simbele, he doesn't seem to be asking me a question, he seems only to be making a statement; so there is no need to answer.

"I believe that we should allow Simbele to try to get the doctor," the leader went on. "Do we all agree?" he asked, but in such a tone that disagreement was impossible—even the man who had accused Moshi of cowardice said nothing, though even in that uncertain light Simbele could see his discontent. Well, thought Simbele, that is what being a leader means; that is what I am not. Once there was a time when a man whom I have now destroyed was that; but he is destroyed and the new man, the one who has no past, is a messenger; yes, a messenger —and I have no desire to challenge this man for his power; I am content to do what he says I should do; and if it was another man who was leader, even if it was the scar-faced man who had no fear for himself or for others, I would be content. Simbele looked across the darkness of the cave and saw that the man was looking at him carefully; steadily he looked back at him, knowing what he was, knowing what he wanted. Did the present leader know too, he wondered, how much this man wanted what he did not have. Once, he remembered, before he had become Simbele, he had wanted the same thing, not because of a love of power, but so that he could do what he was sure was necessary, what the others were afraid to do—and he had taken power, cruelly even, as this man might be cruel, out of belief, not out of desire alone. Did they know what he had been once, he wondered suddenly; had Moshi told them? Was that why this man looked at him so carefully across the cave?

But he forced his mind away from the question, forced himself to know that it did not matter, that it was dead now, that the past was dead, entirely dead.

In the half-darkness, he saw the leader turn to him and heard him say, "You will not have time tonight. We will expect you tomorrow at the same time; with the doctor."

"What will we do if he does not come?" asked the man with the scarred face discontentedly; but the leader did not reply.

* * *

As it happened, there was no need for Simbele to blackmail Redman into tending the wounded terrorist; or, rather, while there seemed to be a need for a time, Simbele, even though he was dealing with a white man over whom he had power, chose not to use blackmail although at first Redman refused to come. Simbele did not hedge at all with Redman; three hours after his return to the settlement, he had gone to Redman's quarters and, finding him still in bed, had waited in his living-room while he washed and dressed. Then he had asked the doctor to dress his injured hand. When they were alone in the surgery, he had said, almost brutally, "Doctor, you have heard that there is a party of terrorists working in the region." Redman had nodded sleepily. Simbele went on, "I am in touch with them . . ." but no, he thought, not the euphemism, the truth: "rather, I am working for them and I have been sent to ask for your assistance." Redman was wide awake now, eyes wide, mouth slightly open both with shock and excitement, forgetting completely about the hand he was tending, so Simbele went straight on. "One of them is badly wounded; he hurt himself cleaning his rifle." Remembering again what he had seen, he gestured towards his face, helplessly—how could you describe that obscene emptiness in words, he wondered. "They have been giving him morphine but that is no good; and they are running out of it. So they want you to go to them to look at the man. If you will come, I will take you tonight."

Redman looked at Simbele then, for a long moment, before bursting out, "Good God man, do you realize what you are asking me?"

"Yes," said Simbele coldly.

"If the police knew, they would shoot me—my God, can you imagine it? WHITE DOCTOR SHOT FOR HELPING TERRORISTS —probably JEWISH DOCTOR SHOT FOR HELPING TERRORISTS."

"Yes," said Simbele; he tried not to show it yet, but inside his head he was sneering at this white man whose first thought was of himself and whose second was of what the newspapers would say. Well, that's it, Simbele said to himself; that's a white liberal at the very heart—everything is fine until it gets dangerous or too public; or perhaps the publicity seems like the best thing to them, the heroic headlines, the sympathetic overseas press. I had thought this one might be different. I had thought there was something extra there: but there isn't—he's just another one of them, another Mrs. Allen, oh so sympathetic —but hollow, as hollow as thunder without rain.

Redman stood up and walked to the window, where he stood looking out for several moments; then, he said, without turning back, "I am, in a way, deeply honoured that you should even ask me. I had not realized that the black people here trusted me to that extent." He swung suddenly back round to face Simbele. "You know what you are doing, I suppose. You realise that by telling me even this you have put yourself completely into my power," and he turned away again. Simbele was sneering openly now, but Redman didn't seem to notice, for he went on. "I won't use that power," he said, "but I'm afraid that I am not going to come. I am tempted to, but I'm afraid I can't. You see, it doesn't matter so much to me alone, but if anything went wrong, it would completely destroy my parents. They simply could not understand." He turned again and looked at Simbele. "I'm sorry, Mr. Simbele, but I won't come. Do you understand? Understand why, I mean?"

Simbele got to his feet; now was the time to use his own power—it would be so easy against this most complete of egoists. Did he understand? Oh yes, he understood—the virtuous doctor had not cared about his parents when he was fucking a black girl; that would have broken them up just as badly, if it had become known. But he knew that he would not use blackmail; it would be like using a sledgehammer to kill an insect. He simply shrugged and left the room.

Four hours later, in the middle of one of his classes, Redman had come to the classroom and told Simbele that he had changed his mind. Even that, thought Simbele, was typical: he had marched into the classroom and up to the desk, right in the middle of a lesson, had leaned forward and whispered to Simbele, "I've changed my mind. I'll tell you later why. I'll meet you at your hut at 9.30 tonight. Will that be enough time?" and Simbele, conscious of the curiosity of the whole class centred on them, had nodded; the moment Redman left he had said, "The doctor just wanted to tell me that a medical test I had for TB was negative." They would understand that, he knew, for all of them had had to have a test after one of their class-mates had been found by Dr. Redman to be tubercular and had been sent off to a special hospital. They had seemed satisfied with the explanation and had gone back to their books; but wasn't that typical, thought Simbele. He wouldn't have thought his behaviour looked odd to the children—he was a white man and they were only children, black children. Well, he would learn something that night, the white man would.

So, while they were walking the eight or so miles to the Narrow Tooth gorge, Simbele had great pleasure in not allowing Redman to explain his reasons for changing his mind. "You must keep quiet," he said. "After all, you yourself told me what would happen to you if you were found doing this." Deliberately, he set a fast pace and was discomfited to find that Redman not only kept up with him, but also caught his arm once when he stumbled and would have fallen.

But, for all his anger at Redman's white egocentricity, Simbele could not help admiring the white man's manner when they at last arrived in the terrorists' cave; he was completely detached and professional, treating the Africans as if they were any group of patients' friends and only momentarily allowing himself to glance at the cases of ammunition and the rifles stacked against the wall of the cave. Before he even looked at the injured man he wanted to wash his hands; he turned to the man nearest him and said, "I shall need water to wash my hands and to clean the patient with," and the man fetched a flask, waited while Redman took the soap from Simbele's haversack, to which he had transferred some of his medical equipment before leaving the settlement, and washed his hands carefully under the water that the man poured from the flask. He handed the soap to Simbele and said, "Will you wash too, please? I shall need someone to hand me instruments." Then he began.

Afterwards Simbele could remember little of what happened during the next half hour. He saw Redman give the man an injection into a vein, he saw Redman begin to cut the dirty bandages away from the man's mutilated head, he saw him direct Moshi to hold the torch so that it shone directly on the face, he saw the torch fall and heard men helping Moshi from the cave and watched as another man took his place. He had to look at the various things that Redman pointed to when he needed them; but he kept his eyes fixed carefully on the wall above the man's head all the rest of the time. Somewhere below the line of his vision he could see the shining instruments as they moved over the blackness of what he did not dare see; and he could hear Dr. Redman's furious breathing, like a man in a race; and he could smell. But his mind he closed away, and time he closed away, and feelings he closed away; and if his senses still worked, it was because he could not help himself away from them.

At last Dr. Redman leaned back from his kneeling position above the man, and said, "Well, that's as much as I can do, here at any rate." Now at last Simbele dared to look at the man; he was decently bandaged now, in the clean white bandages with the distinctive markings of the settlement that Mrs. Allen had had the nurses embroider; but even bandages could not hide the vision of mutilation that Simbele still saw and quickly he looked again at the clean straight lines of the rocks of the caves behind the man's head, and then away. Dr. Redman was talking to him; he hadn't heard.

"Are you all right, Simbele?" he heard the doctor ask again, and he nodded to show that he was. "I was saying," the doctor continued, "that unless that man is taken immediately to hospital he will die; in a way it is astonishing that he is not dead already. If he had not been drugged so heavily already, he would probably have died of shock by now; but he will die anyway unless we get him to hospital. Will you tell whoever is in charge of these men?"

"There is no need to tell me; I know already," came the voice of the man whom Simbele knew to be leader from the darkness behind Redman; but Redman did not turn to look at him. "Simbele," he said again, "is that clear? This man will die within the next forty-eight hours if he is not put into hospital. And even then he has little chance."

"How little chance?" asked the leader. Dr. Redman answered him, but as though it was Simbele who had asked the question, for he looked at Simbele as he spoke. "Perhaps ten to one—twenty to one more probably. Not that he has much of a future, anyway."

"You realize that it is impossible for us to send him to a hospital," said the leader, and again it seemed that Redman answered not him, but Simbele. "I know that," he said, "but it is my job as a doctor to tell you that he will die unless he goes to hospital. I have done what I can for him. All I can do now is to leave behind some more morphine. Will you give it to whoever has been this man's nurse, Simbele? It is in the haversack. There is also a new hypodermic in there. I must wash my hands again," and he stood up and gestured at the man who had been holding the torch to tip the water for him again.

As they were leaving the cave, Simbele turned to the leader and said, "Where is Moshi?" Another of the men, squatting on the floor of the cave, pointed over to where a man lay sprawled out on the floor. Simbele went over to him. In the light of the hurricane lamp, he could see that he was fast asleep. "He has been awake with the injured one ever since it happened," the leader said quietly to Simbele; and then, even more quietly, as they pushed their way out of the cave on to the ledge, he went on, "I think that Moshi was afraid we would kill him. We knew that he would die, you see. The one who is hurt . . . his name is Boy; he is Moshi's brother."

Standing on the ledge in the darkness, Simbele said nothing. Dr. Redman was already on his way down the cliff in the rough rope harness; while he waited for the three men to pull it back up again, Simbele watched the clear stars and the unclear mass of the Milky Way that spread across the darkness of the night sky.

IX

At first, after the terrible thing that she had seen between Dr. Redman and Nurse Peters, Mrs. Allen decided that what she must do was to confront Dr. Redman and tell him that unless his misbehaviour stopped immediately she would have to report the matter to the Superintendent; but when she actually planned the confrontation in her mind, she realized that she could not possibly act so directly—or, rather, while one of the voices said that the best thing she could do was to act directly, going straight to either Dr. Redman or Nurse Peters, another said that while such directness had its place, this was a time for caution; and yet another cried softly that there was nothing she could do, that she must close her eyes and ears from now on and must be entirely discreet. There were other voices too, voices that sneered and jabbered and laughed grotesquely; but most of the time she managed to keep them under control and even when they spoke to her in her dreams she would force herself to wake up and would silence them angrily.

So, when she acted, she listened to the cautious voice, and she began to watch; she didn't go near Redman's house again, but she watched; she watched Dr. Redman in the hospital; she watched Nurse Peters; she watched the way they looked at each other; she watched the way the other nurses spoke to Dr. Redman, the way they looked at him, the way he looked at them; and she saw things that she had not seen before, and she heard things—saw the way in which the doctor managed to brush close to the nurses when he went past them in the ward, saw his eyes moving over their rounded bodies underneath the starched blue uniforms, saw even how, once or twice when he thought he wasn't being observed, he surreptitiously fondled their breasts and behinds—and it was not only Nurse Peters, it was the other nurses too; and she noted how they giggled quietly in their room, how they smiled coyly at him when he passed them, how sometimes they seemed deliberately to put themselves where he could brush close to them, almost as if they were teasing him. For a time she thought of sacking Nurse Peters; but it was obvious that it wasn't only her, and if she went she would simply be replaced by another. It would be easy enough to do—she could find fault with Nurse Peters's work, could provoke her to rudeness, and then demand that she be sacked; she was very tempted to do that; but it would only allow Dr. Redman to corrupt yet another person.

But what she could do was to make it difficult for Nurse Peters to get to Dr. Redman's house at certain times. So, for two afternoons, she found additional work for her to do that would keep her in the wards; and she went to check that the work was being properly done, that Nurse Peters had not slipped away; but on the third afternoon, when she was sure that Nurse Peters must be in the wards, scrubbing the floor that Mrs. Allen had said had not been done properly, and when she was sitting in the armchair in her bedroom, an armchair that she had almost unconsciously placed so that she could watch Redman's house from her window, she woke suddenly from her half-doze because she was almost sure that she had seen someone in the blue uniform of the nurses, slip surreptitiously in through the back door of Redman's house. Quickly Mrs. Allen got up and went to the hospital; if Nurse Peters were not there, she knew where she would be—and she would have to sack her, since she was avoiding a set job. But when she got to the hospital, she found that there was a nurse there scrubbing the already spotless floor. "Where is Nurse Peters?" she demanded of the nurse, who lifted her soapy hands from the floor, smiled, said, "She was tired; she asked me to do this for her so that she could go home to rest," and then, as Mrs. Allen was leaving the ward, giggled in such a way that Mrs. Allen stopped and turned sharply back to her; the nurse looked straight at her and giggled again, before starting to scrub again, singing quietly to herself.

Perhaps they know, thought Mrs. Allen; perhaps they know that I know—perhaps they even think that I am a willing participant in this filth. Looking at the girl, bent forward on her knees, with her skirt tucked up so that her thighs showed, she had suddenly a memory of what she had seen three days before, the urgent thrusting, the sensuality, the filth involved in loving without love. Almost running, she returned to her own bedroom, where she pulled her armchair closer to the window so that she could see Redman's house better; she was tempted to go straight to the house, to bang on the door until Redman came to answer, to push her way in and to discover Nurse Peters hiding somewhere, probably naked, in his bedroom, or to go again to the window of the bedroom so that she could have renewed evidence. But the voice of the cautious one held her in the chair; and when half an hour later she saw Nurse Peters come quietly out of the back door of Redman's house and make her way back towards the hospital, she knew that now she must act, that she must ignore all the voices except that which said, You must see Dr. Redman; you must tell him that unless this behaviour stops immediately, you will inform the Superintendent; and Dr. Redman will know what that means. She forced silence upon the other voices, which told her variously to do this, that, the other, not to care; and she ignored that other voice which said things that were too terrible to bear, that voice which became her own self sometimes in the dreams that she did not dare remember.

She tried to see Redman that night, but he left the dinner table earlier than usual, before the Superintendent even, saying that he had work to do in the hospital; so she went home and sat in the armchair in her dark bedroom and waited for the lights to go on in his house, so that she could go to him. But when, after a while, they didn't, she walked over to the hospital; he wasn't there either—Sister Mbele, who was on duty, told her that although Dr. Redman had come in and had spent ten minutes in the dispensary, he had left then and she did not know where he was; wasn't he in bed? she asked. So Mrs. Allen went to his house, which was still unlit, and knocked at the door; but he didn't come and she could see through the curtains of his bedroom that he didn't seem to be there. His car was in the lean-to garage next to his house, so he could not have gone to town. Then Mrs. Allen was quite sure that she knew where he was: he was in the fields somewhere, probably with Nurse Peters, perhaps with one of the other nurses, perhaps with some other young pretty girl from the settlement, doing what was impossible to think about.

She went home and sat in the armchair in her bedroom, waiting for him to come back. But when he hadn't come at two o'clock, she fell asleep, and dreamt terrible dreams, and woke at dawn, still sitting in the armchair, with her dress creased and smelly, and her limbs cold and stiff.

She found him alone later that morning, sitting at the small desk in the dispensary in the hospital. As she came in, he looked up and she saw, with disgust, that his eyes were bloodshot and his face puffy, the very look of excess, she thought. But before she could speak, he gave her exactly the chance she had been looking for.

"I'm glad to have a moment to talk to you, Mrs. Allen," he said. "I'm afraid to say that I have had a complaint from the nurses that you are treating Nurse Peters unfairly," and when she started to speak, he stopped her and went on; "Mrs. Allen, no doubt you have reason to think that Nurse Peters is not working well; but if that is so, do you not think that we should ask her to leave, to find some other employment, rather than trying to make her work harder?"

That's it, thought Mrs. Allen; that's the last proof I need. What I saw happening between you and Nurse Peters wasn't love—if it had been, you could not so callously suggest that we sack her. Now I am certain that you weren't with her last night; it was probably some new one, some pretty young black girl from the settlement whom you have already corrupted; and when I sack Nurse Peters, you will suggest that we take this new one in as her replacement. Then you will be able to watch her with your leering eyes, as you watch me now. She had to act, she knew.

"Dr. Redman, the only complaint I have is one that concerns you more than anyone."

Suddenly angry, he stood up, and said, "If you have any complaints about the way in which I do my job, I suggest that you convey them to the Superintendent." He went over to his dispensing cupboard and began shifting bottles and bandages and ointments around almost aimlessly, then swung round at her and said, furiously, "Who the hell do you think you are, anyway? Do you think that because you have some obscure relationship with some obscure missionary who once worked here you can take over the settlement, as if you had a spiritual right to the place?"

"Dr. Allen founded the settlement; he wasn't obscure, he had a world-reputation—and anyway, having been married to his grandson doesn't give me any rights, as you think; it gives me responsibility, that's all."

"Responsibility? For what? For interference in our lives?"

"If necessary, yes," she said. "Certainly I have a responsibility to stop you corrupting the people of the settlement."

"What on earth are you talking about? What do you mean, 'corrupting'?" Dr. Redman appeared now, for the first time, to be genuinely puzzled; he looks at me, thought Mrs. Allen, as if

I were out of my mind—and for a moment her sense of purpose deserted her, and she could not connect what was happening outside her mind with the rabble of voices that jabbered and shrieked inside—but it was in having that purpose that she knew her salvation lay; it was when Terry spoke inside her mind that she knew what she had to do.

"Look, Dr. Redman, there is no point in your pretending; I know all about you—I know about you and the nurses, I know what you have been doing with Nurse Peters, I saw what you were doing, I saw that . . . that . . . that . . ." She could hear herself that her voice was becoming hysterical; she could hear somewhere inside her a high-pitched cackling laughter, the laughter of old Joseph as he placed flowers on Dr. Allen's grave. Hold on to yourself, Terry's voice cried inside her, hold on; you are right, this thing must be done, it has to be done—and she knew that what she had said had made Dr. Redman know that she knew, that she must know for, first, he stood, very still, next to the dispensing cupboard, and then he walked back to his desk and sat down again, as if he did not trust himself to stand.

"I don't know what on earth you are talking about, Mrs. Allen; if you mean what I think you mean, all I can say is that you have no evidence."

"I have the evidence of my own eyes," she cried out in rage that he continued the pretence.

"Then you are deluded," he said flatly.

"Stop pretending, Dr. Redman; stop pretending. I tell you, I saw; I saw what you were doing." She leaned forward, with both her hands on the edge of the desk, and then went on speaking very quietly, "Do you remember that afternoon, when Mrs. Madele's baby was in spasm, and I came to get you? You do remember, don't you? Well, before I knocked at the door, I went round to your bedroom window to see if you were awake —I think I heard voices, you see, that made me know what you were doing." Now her voice was triumphant; she had him held in her power, she knew. "I saw what you and Nurse Peters were doing. I saw with my own eyes through your bedroom window."

"If you saw that, why didn't you go for the police—or tell the Superintendent, which would be just about the same thing?" He was watching her eyes and she did not dare look away.

"No," she almost whispered. "You know that I can't do that. You'd go to prison; they'd stop you being a doctor; I might as well kill you."

"Yes," he said slowly. "You might. And kill Nurse Peters at the same time."

"I'm not going to the police, Dr. Redman; I told you that."

"What are you going to do about this thing that you think you saw then?"

"I am asking you to stop it," and because that was not strong enough, she added, "telling you to stop corrupting Nurse Peters and, as far as I can tell, the other nurses too."

"And if I refuse to stop what you call 'corrupting' them?" he sneered at her.

"Then I shall have to tell the Superintendent."

"Which, as I told you before, is as good as going to the police."

"I don't care about that," she said. "I have to stop it somehow . . ." her voice trailed away.

"Oh, the Superintendent would love that; he'd get the police, and sack me, and give evidence against me, and you'd have to give evidence against me—and can't you just see the newspaper headlines, *Young Jewish Doctor on Immorality Charge*, with special emphasis on the *Jewish*?" he spat out. Then, almost as if he were remembering something that he did not want to remember, he brought a hand up to his mouth, and his eyes widened, and his face grew whiter even under the pallor of tiredness. While she watched him, watched what she thought were the implications of the power which she now held over him sinking into his consciousness, he stood up, still staring at her with widened eyes, turned his back and walked to the window, where he looked out over the hazy dust-greyed air of noon.

"Do you know where I come from, Mrs Allen?" he said, after a moment. She nodded, but he could not see. "I come from Sea Point, where my parents run a small . . . restaurant, they call it, but it is really a café; and they sell just about everything that the law allows them to sell—and Sea Point is a pretty wealthy area, you know, but they have never quite made the grade, perhaps because they are so unadventurous. It was quite a struggle for them, to send me to be a doctor, six years it was and they never talked about money, but I know that they skimped themselves, and their clothes got shabbier and shabbier, and the car got old and used to break down every time they went more than ten miles. But they thought it would be all right, you see; I'd be a doctor and set up a good practice in the Cape and make a lot of money. Then, when I qualified, and told them that I wanted to do this job, they couldn't really understand, but they didn't say anything to stop me." He swung round at Mrs. Allen. "Did your husband know that when he wrote to Professor Abrahams? And wasn't he a little disappointed that he couldn't find a Christian doctor?" Mrs. Allen said nothing; she could remember so clearly what Terry had said, it was almost as if he were still speaking inside her head: "Well, it is a pity," he had said, "that we can't get a Christian; I'm not being anti-Semitic, because I'm grateful to this young man—but it is still a pity." But he hadn't meant what Dr. Redman thought he meant; that kind of narrow Christians they had never been, she and Terry; their Christianity had been a matter of the way you behaved, not what you said you believed—and what would disgust Terry about this man would not be what he said, but that he acted without love, used the manner of love without meaning it.

Dr. Redman was looking at her still, puzzled by her silence; then he turned away again and began to talk again. "You see, Mrs. Allen, I felt that I had to come somewhere where I would not be well paid, where I would not be comfortable, where my parents would not be there to get me out of any difficulty, where I would have to work with third-rate equipment and untrained assistants. I hadn't calculated on one thing, though; I hadn't realized that I'd get lonely—I thought I could manage on my own, I thought I had enough inside me to be self-sufficient; I just hadn't calculated on loneliness."

"You don't have to tell me anything about loneliness," Mrs. Allen whispered across the room.

Sneering again, he swung round at her. "Nonsense," he said. "You want me to think that you're a poor widow woman, entirely on your own. Well, you don't fool me; because I know, everyone knows, that you aren't lonely. You live in a world of the dead. Do you think we don't see you, when you go up there," and he gestured towards the cemetery, "to wander around the graves? Do you think that everyone in the settlement doesn't laugh at the way you talk to yourself up there? 'Oh my dear Terry,' " he mimicked her voice cruelly, " 'oh my dear Terry, what shall I do without you? But you won't ever leave me, will you? You promise you won't leave?' You are sick, Mrs. Allen; you might as well be dead."

"How dare you?" she screamed at him. "How dare you, you revolting little . . . dirt, you filth."

"Why don't you call me a Jew, Mrs. Allen? That's what you are thinking," and then, suddenly, as if he had made up his mind about something, he walked back to his seat and sat down, leaning back in his chair, a hand under his chin, in a caricature of the professional manner. "Tell me, as a doctor," he emphasized "doctor" heavily, "isn't it true that the direct cause of your present outburst—particularly with its references to dirt and filth—is your," and he leaned forward so that she could not miss a syllable of what he said, "sexual frustration." He leaned back again and even his pretence at the professional manner could not keep the smile of triumph from his face.

Inside her head the voices were screaming in panic and fury and terror, a rabble of wild voices which leapt and twisted and cavorted in the dust and which bore down on her and swept her away. Slowly she raised her hands to cover her mouth and, with their protection, she was at last able to select one of the voices and let it speak. "No," the voice whispered. "No, that's not true, it's not true."

"Oh," said Redman, flatly. "Well, how about this for an explanation? You are suffering from guilt, because you never really enjoyed sex with your husband, and you feel that if you had given him more of what he wanted, he would not have died."

"Oh God," the voice whispered from behind the hands that now covered all her face. "Oh God."

Dr. Redman crossed the room to where she was standing. He grabbed her by each wrist and forced her hands away from her face, forced her arms apart, pulling them upwards so that she whimpered with the pain. "Look at me," he said, harshly. "You can go to the police with this story about Nurse Peters and me. Yes, you can go to them. Do you know what my defence will be? That you are suffering from delusions brought about by the sexual frustration of being a widow. And I'll do something else too—I'll tell the police that you have brought this charge against me after you had made indecent suggestions to me, which I refused to entertain; so you decided to fabricate these charges about Nurse Peters and me. They may not believe me, of course; they may even convict me and send me to prison. But I won't care, you see; because you will be finished, you will be worse 'dirt' than I am." He let her wrists go, so that her arms dropped to her sides; automatically, she rubbed the red weals on her wrists that the pressure of his grasp had caused. He stepped back from her two or three paces and then said, with a strange little smile on his lips, "And then, with you worse than dirt, I . . ." he smiled still, ". . . I shall kill myself. I could not bear to hurt my parents by staying alive; and they would be able to feel sorrier for me as a dead immoralist than as a living convict. You see, Mrs. Allen; I am a doctor—I'm not afraid of dying, even though I don't particularly want to die yet; and I'd die easily, with a handful of barbiturates, a syringe of air pumped into a vein, a scalpel across the throat or the wrists, an overdose of morphine jabbed into my thigh. It'd be so easy for me. Not like you; because you want to die, you want to go to 'darling Terry', but you are afraid that you might not go to him." He was smiling more broadly now, in triumph and cruelty; and Mrs. Allen's hands were over her face again and she was shaking all over, like someone in a fever or demented. "So, Mrs. Allen, go to the police," he commanded, and then, more roughly, "Come on, get out of here—go to the police." Mrs. Allen did not move and so, almost tenderly, he took her by the arm and led her round the desk and made her sit in his chair; and while she sat there, still with her hands over her face, he leaned over beside her and whispered in her ear, "Come now, Mrs. Allen, I was only trying to make you understand; I wasn't trying to hurt you deliberately—I just wanted you to understand. I would kill myself, you know, if you told the police, and so you won't tell them, will you? That's all you have to understand. People like us, you see . . . we're caught; we're trapped—there's no way out for us, only one way. I just wanted you to understand," and when her only response was to begin weeping in great choking spasms of terror, he stood up, saying, "You'll be all right now; cry yourself out now and you'll be all right," and left her to the weeping, screaming, cackling, jibbering voices that nobody but she could hear.

* * *

From that time on, and all the time, Mrs. Allen knew that she was going mad; or she thought so; or she guessed so. There was one of the voices that kept on saying that; she could hear it saying, You are out of your mind, you are mad, you are having what nice people call a nervous breakdown; but the truth is plain—you are going mad; and then another voice would cry, Intolerable, intolerable, intolerable; and then another, Hollow, hollow, hollow; and then she would seek desperately for Terry's voice in her mind, and when she found it, he would be saying the wrong things, he in his kind level voice would be saying worse things than Dr. Redman had said to her; and then she would find, coming unsummoned into her consciousness, the clear enunciation of Simbele speaking words that did not belong to him; and interrupting everything, the senile cackling laughter of old Joseph.

There were moments when she managed to gather her voices together again; as quickly as she could she would sweep them into one of the side rooms of her mind and close the door on them and turn the key. But then she would wander through the empty dusty rooms of the empty dusty house peering in the empty dusty cupboards, and she would, almost by accident, open the wrong door, and the sneering, jabbering, disembodied voices would come swarming back. Frantically she would gather them up again and lock them away; but, after a while, she would not be able to tolerate the emptiness of the house and would cautiously open the locked door and let Terry alone out. But he would open his mouth and speak not in his own voice but in the sneering tones of Simbele, the foulness of Redman, or the cackles of old Joseph. So either she must let them all out and try to control them or she must lock them away and be prepared to live in the complete emptiness.

As always, she tried to save herself by working; it wasn't enough now to tell other people to work, she must work herself. So she would dress herself in overalls and go down on her hands and knees on the floor of the hospital wards and scrub and scrub and polish and polish until her hands could hardly hold the cloths and her knees were bruised; but still she would hear the voices and so she would have to stop her work and she would go walking round the settlement, peering into the classroom, peering into the huts of the Africans, peering through the windows of Redman's cottage; and she would walk up to the cemetery and watch old Joseph as he dug his graves and tended his paths and laid flowers on his father's grave. Then she would walk back to the hospital and stand to watch Redman as he worked at his desk or dispensed to outpatients or tended the people in the wards.

For, when the voices were closed away from her mind, she seemed to develop a strange dependence on Dr. Redman, as a child might whose father had left the home and who had now to accept as father a new man, someone she did not know, someone whom she was suspicious of, but someone whom she needed to understand. She would stand to watch him with uncomprehending but curious eyes, watching him carefully, as if in the movements of his hands there was a clue to his presence. At first he found her disturbing and several times told her so bluntly; but she did not seem to understand. He knew perfectly well that she was in the early stages of what might be a serious breakdown; but when he went to the Superintendent to tell him that something should be done, all the Superintendent said was, "Well, it doesn't surprise me; I warned the Bishop that she did not sound the right person. But there is nothing I can do; you are the doctor—can't you give her something to calm her down?" So Dr. Redman gave her regular sedatives; and she seemed to be all right again, for she began to bully the nurses again, and to have bright ideas for the re-organization of the hospital, and for the settlement generally; they would even talk, he sitting at his desk while she did the difficult darning that she could not trust Sister Mbele to cope with. Mrs. Allen would talk quite naturally and relaxedly about her life before she came to the settlement, about her dead husband and his family, about the school he had been headmaster of, about the long low white-washed buildings that lay just below the line of the Drakensberg timber lands, about Caroline and her husband Charles, about Peter, about the successes of some of the children they had looked after and about the failures; and Dr. Redman would talk, as naturally as she did, about his parents, his childhood in Sea Point, his life at university, his ambitions for the future; until suddenly he would become aware that she had stopped her work and that she was listening to him but was not hearing him, was staring at him with those uncomprehending but curious eyes, as if she were asleep and dreaming. So he would keep silent and then after a few moments she would seem to recover herself again and would be able to pay attention to what happened outside her rather than to whatever was going on inside her head.

X

There was fighting in the mountains that week. You could hear the rifles and machine-guns in the settlement as if it had been only a hundred yards away. When Simbele in his classroom heard the shooting, he left the part of the class he was teaching English to and walked over to the open window and listened; the class behind was very quiet and he knew that they were listening too. He heard someone push his chair back and stand up suddenly and he turned round to see the slow Petrus standing, fists clenched and mouth working. "Sit down, Petrus," he said. "Sit down and get on with your work," and, acknowledging almost for the first time that anyone else felt what he felt, and not caring that the whole class heard him, "There is nothing that we can do."

The shooting went on for half an hour and then, quite unexpectedly, stopped; ten minutes later there was another brief outburst and then again it stopped. That was all.

But at lunchtime news reached the settlement that the police had lost touch with the main body of the terrorists. They had killed three of them for a loss of one of their own men, with one badly wounded and one slightly; and now, while the main body of police went on looking for the terrorists in the mountains, a small group of policemen were driving around from farm to farm in the valley, taking with them the bodies of the three terrorists whom they had killed, in the hope of being able to identify them and so have some clue about likely hiding places of the rest. The people of the settlement heard that much from a farm labourer who came cycling past in the early afternoon on his way to Verderdorp; and then, an hour or two later, Simbele himself heard from Petrus, who had rushed off the moment morning school had ended and who had, on a borrowed bicycle, actually managed to get to one of the neighbouring farms while the identification parade of the dead terrorists was still in progress, and who had managed to get into conversation with one of the black policemen, what had happened that morning.

The police had been on one of the routine scouting expeditions along the foot of the mountains that they had been conducting since the attack on the farm and the ambush of the rescue force. They had seen a suspicious character in the thick brush near the mouth of the Narrow Tooth gorge (Petrus looked significantly at Simbele when he gave the name) and had chased him in their land-rovers until it seemed they might lose him, when one of the white policemen had shot him down. As two policemen had gone through the brush to collect the body, two or three men, concealed in the rocks above the gorge, one armed with a sub-machine gun, had opened fire and had killed one of the policemen and wounded the other. The other policeman had taken cover behind the land-rovers, had radioed for help and, while they were waiting for it to arrive, had returned the fire; then, after half an hour, the two or three terrorists had retired. After waiting a while, since they suspected a trap, the police had collected their wounded man and the dead one, put them in a land-rover, left one man to look after them, and had followed the terrorists. Half a mile into the rough country of the mountains, they had been halted again by another terrorist with an automatic rifle; but alone he had not been able to pin them down and so one of the policemen had been able to get round to the side of him and shoot him. When they got to him, Petrus explained quietly to Simbele, they found that he had been guarding the dead body of another terrorist, who had been shot some time before (and Petrus gestured at his own jaw to explain the injury) and who had probably been dead before the attack started. Petrus stopped his story there, abruptly, and looked at Simbele as if he expected him to say something; but Simbele said nothing and turned away from Petrus and walked back towards the classroom.

Four policemen, two white and two black, arrived later that afternoon. They drew their land-rover truck up in the middle of the dust-bowl of the settlement and, while the more senior of the white policemen went in to the office of the Superintendent, the black men walked round the camp, calling on the people to assemble in the bowl; there was no need for them to call, really, for people had begun moving from their huts the moment the van stopped. Simbele, however, went on teaching his class, despite the children's restlessness, until a policeman walked in without knocking, ordered him to stop teaching and the children and Simbele to assemble with the others.

When everybody was there, the white people too, Dr. Redman protesting at being disturbed in his surgery, Mrs. Allen as quiet as she had been ever since her confrontation with Dr. Redman, and the Superintendent, armed with his revolver and looking like a minor version of the policeman by whose side he walked, the senior policeman ordered one of the black policemen to open the back of the truck. This he did and then, as roughly as if he had been handling bags of mealie meal, he pulled, one by one, the three bodies out of the back of the truck and on to the ground. The crowd stirred and one woman near Simbele half-cried out in indignation but was silenced by her neighbours. The policemen then forced the crowd back a few paces and, entirely at random it seemed, picked people from the crowd to come forward and forced each one to look at the bodies; the response was always the same, a short stare and a sullen shake of the head, even when the police called on one of the pupils who had, Simbele knew, seen Moshi when he first came to the settlement. For he had known, almost so certainly that he had not needed to look, that one of the dead men would be Moshi and that one would be the man whom Redman had tended; he couldn't recognize the other man, who wasn't, in fact, dressed in the same para-military gear that Moshi and his brother were wearing, but in the dirty blue overalls of any farm labourer—he was probably a farm labourer anyway, thought Simbele, not a terrorist at all, who had panicked at the sight of the land-rovers and had been shot for running away, not for anything else.

The police were, by now, obviously not expecting to find anyone willing to identify the dead men, for, though they continued to call individuals from the crowd and to force them to look, they chose those who looked frightened anyway or those who looked too indignant or sullen. Suddenly, Mrs. Allen, standing near the Superintendent, pushed her way through the crowd of black people and forward into the open space. Brushing past the policemen, she stooped down over the bodies; as she did so, Simbele suddenly remembered something from his nightmare vision of the cave—there was something wrong there, something that did not fit, something that he could see in front of him, something to do with those bodies, something that he should have been able to see in the cave but which hadn't then been able to break through the horror of his upper mind, but something which was now hovering on the edge of his consciousness—and as Mrs. Allen put a hand down towards the mutilated head of Moshi's brother, he remembered: what was wrong was those bandages, and what was wrong with them was that every single one of them had embroidered on it, in small, neat stitching, the initials "S J S", St. Joseph's Settlement. And was it that Mrs. Allen was there for? Was it that which made her stretch a hand slowly out to the dead man?

But, as the crowd watched her, all Mrs. Allen did was to close, very gently, the eyes of each of the dead men lying in the dust. The police were so surprised that they did not have time to stop her and, when the junior policeman pushed her away from the bodies and asked what the devil she thought she was doing, she answered loudly, so that everyone in the crowd could hear, "I don't care what these men have done; you have no right to treat the dead with disrespect." The crowd sighed then, as a forest does before a storm comes; and the white policemen had drawn their revolvers and the Superintendent had stepped quickly out of the crowd to join them, though he was too afraid to draw his own revolver and could only whisper curses at Mrs. Allen. But the crowd did not move and when the black policemen, on the orders of the senior white policeman, told them to disperse immediately, the people turned quietly and moved away to their huts on the edge of the dust-bowl. Mrs. Allen began to weep then, standing a few yards away from the dead bodies and the policemen and the Superintendent, who by now had managed to draw his revolver and was waving it excitedly at the disappearing people; and Simbele looking round as he walked away across the dust-bowl had seen Sister Mbele come forward and take Mrs. Allen by the arm and lead her, still weeping, back across the dust-bowl towards her cottage.

* * *

Later, in the early dusk, Mrs. Allen left her cottage again and walked up to the cemetery, where she took three of the white Barberton daisies that old Joseph put on Dr. Allen's grave that morning. She walked back down to the dust-bowl to the place where, from the marks in the dust, you could tell that the bodies had lain. Very carefully she placed one flower in each place that a body had been and then went quietly away again. Simbele, standing in the door of his hut watching the same place as the dusk came down, saw Mrs. Allen coming and saw that she placed something there, but could not see what; he did not go to investigate, for he was half-expecting Redman to come to see him that evening—he felt sure that Redman must by now have realized the mistake that they had made with the bandages; but when it was dark and Redman had not come, he left his hut and went to the classroom where he prepared his lessons for the next day.

* * *

The police came back to the settlement later that night again, four of them, but now three white and one black, driving carefully into the settlement and going straight to the Superintendent's office, so that no one except him and his houseboy knew that they were there. After the three white policemen had spent about a quarter of an hour there, the Superintendent sent his houseboy to fetch Mrs. Allen.

The houseboy, who slept in a small room behind the Superintendent's house, found Mrs. Allen in her cottage; he did not even have to knock, for she was standing in the open door of the unlighted front room, staring out across the dust-bowl. "Mrs. Allen," he said, "the man—" he jerked his head in the vague direction of the Superintendent's cottage, but Mrs. Allen knew whom he meant; all the Africans used that phrase for him —"the man says you must come."

Without asking why, she followed him across the dusty space to the Superintendent's office. The houseboy opened the door for her and then scuttled away around the side of the house; she shut the door carefully behind her and stood quietly in the dark hallway. She could hear men's voices in the front room but, when she tried to hear what they were saying, she realized that they were talking in Afrikaans and she could not understand; the door to the room wasn't completely closed, so, still standing in the hallway, she gave it a little push so that it swung open. The four men inside looked round to stare at her, in silence. Then one of the policemen, a Major from the look of his uniform, made a gesture to the Superintendent, who said, "Come in, Mrs. Allen. The police here have a few questions they want to ask you." Mrs. Allen did not move. The Major gestured again and the Superintendent said, more curtly even this time, "Come on, Mrs. Allen."

From somewhere out of the past a voice spoke with her mouth: "Is it the custom of the police—and you too, Superintendent—not to rise when a woman comes into the room?"

One of the younger policemen made a movement as if he were going to stand but when another spoke to him, angrily in Afrikaans, he sat again. Mrs. Allen looked at the man who had tried to stand—she knew him; he was the one who usually visited the settlement on the routine inspections that the police made to all the farms of the valley and to the settlement. "Good evening, Sergeant," she said. "I am glad to see that your upbringing at least has not deserted you. As for you," turning to the other policeman, the man who had stopped the Sergeant standing, "If I were a younger woman I would slap your face."

"Sergeant Van Wyk would hit you back, Mrs. Allen," said the Major. He spoke in the manner of an educated man; his English was nearly faultless—only the slightly guttural intonation revealed that he was not English by birth—and he smiled, ironically, as he spoke.

Mrs. Allen was still standing; now she looked at the Major. She had to wait a moment or two before she spoke; it took time to select Terry's voice from the others which crowded her head—but she knew that was the right voice to choose: Terry would know how to cope with this situation; Terry would know—and Terry was speaking with her voice, and Terry was telling her, Don't be afraid of these despicable men. Don't be afraid of what Dr. Redman said he would do. Don't be afraid. No one would blame you for keeping silent about what you know; and if the police make you admit what you know, nobody will blame you for keeping silent, especially since you did try to stop it. Don't be afraid, my darling, don't be afraid.

But she was afraid; she had to close her eyes before Terry's words would come to her. "I think it despicable of you," the words came, "to avoid using your authority over these men to make them rise when a woman enters their presence." She opened her eyes again; the Major smiled and leaned back in his chair. "Sergeant," he said, "perhaps you will give a chair to Mrs. Allen."

Before she had sat herself down properly, Sergeant Van Wyk asked her the first question; before she had time to answer, the other sergeant asked her another, more politely, more gently. She began to answer this one, when Sergeant Van Wyk snapped at her, "Answer my question, Mrs. Allen." She hesitated, looking from one to the other, not daring to speak, because the questions were muddling in her mind, and she couldn't find the words to answer with. She looked at the Superintendent; he was looking at the desk; the Major was smiling at her still, coldly, with half-closed eyes. "Answer Sergeant Van Wyk's question first," said the other sergeant; he spoke almost as a friend would, and smiled gently at her. "All right," she said, looking at him, then turning to Sergeant Van Wyk, "All right."

The questions were trivial; how long had she been at the settlement? Where had she been before? Why had she come here? What was her work? How many nurses did she have under her? What kind of school had her husband been headmaster of? What children did she have? She could answer all of them easily enough, just by letting Terry's quiet voice suggest the words to her. Answer honestly, he said; give them details. Don't be afraid. All these are just trivial questions; they will come to the difficult ones later. Only once did she search for Terry's words and not find them, and that was when the friendly sergeant asked her, "How long has your husband been dead, Mrs. Allen?"

"Dead?" she said—suddenly her body seemed to be shaking, her hands, head, mind, all shaking, as if in some sudden fever. "Terry? Dead?" she asked, just as she had asked her daughter when she had broken the news to her in the hospital that Terry had died five minutes before, very peacefully. "Terry's not dead," she said. "I know he's not dead; what died in there didn't matter—he's not dead," and she smiled the same brilliant smile at the sergeant that she had smiled at her daughter then, the smile that had made her daughter take the doctor aside to ask for sedatives for her mother, to tide her over the shock. Now, both sergeants turned to the Major to seek his advice; even the policeman who had been taking notes of all the questions and her answers looked up from his notebook for the first time. The Major turned to the Superintendent, who leaned forward to whisper in his ear, and then signalled at the sergeants to continue their questioning.

As the questions went on, and as they became less and less connected with what she thought the police had come to question her about, Mrs. Allen grew more and more puzzled. There had not been one question about Dr. Redman yet, not one question about Nurse Peters; they would, she was sure, get round to that sooner or later—she didn't know how they knew about it, she didn't know how they knew about her knowing about that, but they must know: why else should they be questioning her at all? But then again, these questions did not seem to bear any relation to the other thing, the terrible thing; perhaps they were only trying to confuse her, perhaps they were trying to make her afraid—and she was afraid, but Terry was there, and he would not allow her to be afraid. As long as she had him there, she was safe; and didn't he keep telling her to wait, to wait, to wait, not to try to hurry the questions along, because as soon as she did try that, the police would know what she did not want to tell them? So she answered the questions, carefully, pausing for a moment to allow herself time to sort out what it was that Terry wanted her to answer. The world was reduced to that small circle, the friendly question from one sergeant, the deliberate pause, the answer; the unkind question from the other, the pause, another careful answer; again and again.

So, when the circle was broken, when the Major interrupted the sergeants suddenly to say, "Now we come to an important question, Mrs. Allen. I want to know why you interfered with my men this afternoon," she took a moment or two to focus her eyes on him; he seemed to be so far away, he seemed so far outside the circle on which all her concentration had been fixed, that she lost Terry in the crowds of jabbering voices and in panic had to search for him, search for him, opening doors, peering into the darkness, seeing nobody, hearing only the voices, multitudinous. Then it was all right, then he came back, to help her; and she could say what she had said after he had told her what she must do, this afternoon; "I don't care what those men were or what they had done; your men had no right to treat the dead with such disrespect."

Sergeant Van Wyk was on his feet, shouting at her: "disrespect? Disrespect?" he raged. "Do you want us to show respect for those foulnesses, those murdering bastards?"

Sergeant Van der Post, still more controlled, more urbane, said too, before she had time to find the right words to answer: "come, Mrs. Allen; now surely you don't mean that. After all, you know what those men did. You know what they did to Mrs. Van Breda and to her daughter."

Mrs. Allen stared at him; the name meant nothing to her. "Come, Mrs. Allen," the sergeant coaxed. "You know the farmer's wife who the terrorists raped and then mutilated."

She nodded; she knew about it—it had been in the dream, not the one before she knew, but the one afterwards. She had heard about it at dinner from Dr. Redman, who had read it from a newspaper; and she had dreamt it, every part of it. She knew what he meant. Had those men done it, she wondered.

Those men hadn't been the men in her dream; they were different, she remembered—the men she knew about had been in her dream; they had been in the crowd this afternoon; she had kept away from them; they hadn't been the three men dead in the dust, whose eyes she had closed. "How do you know it was those men?" she asked.

"You see, she does mean it," Sergeant Van Wyk said to his colleague. "She is as bad as they are. She probably helps them, this one. Don't you, Mrs. Allen—" he sneered the name—"don't you help them? You with your fine ideas about respect; you helped them."

"Don't be silly," said Sergeant Van der Post. "Of course she didn't help them. You didn't help them, did you Mrs. Allen?"

"No," she said.

"Then why does she talk about respect?" Sergeant Van Wyk asked.

"Why do you talk all this nonsense about respect, Mrs. Allen?" the friendly sergeant asked. "After all, there is certain evidence that they were the terrorists—there can't be any doubt about it; and you know what they did, not only to the Van Bredas but to the policemen."

"I am not saying that I approve of what they did; of course I don't; I'm just saying that everyone deserves to be treated with respect."

"You see," said Sergeant Van Wyk, as if he were accusing his colleague of having said what Mrs. Allen said, "You see, she is not prepared to condemn those bastards; she is making excuses for them."

"That is not true, Sergeant Van Wyk; she means . . ." Sergeant Van der Post was acting his role carefully still; he paused now, almost in the way Mrs. Allen did before she answered a question, and then said, as if he were genuinely puzzled, "Just what do you mean, Mrs. Allen? Are you not prepared to condemn them?"

Again she paused, seeking for the right words: "Of course I condemn them; I condemn all violence."

"Yet you were prepared to help them." This was out of the circle again; this was the Major speaking. She looked across the distance of the room at him; what he had said had emptied her mind—she was shocked into being herself again, into speaking with her own words in her own voice. "What do you mean?" she asked. "I don't know what on earth you are talking about."

The Major stood now; he came round the table quickly at her, bending down to roar in her face; "You know, Mrs. Allen, you know all right. You were prepared to help them." He thrust his face right close to hers; she could not help it but she had to pull back into her chair, away from this coarse face, these cold eyes, this hot dirty breath. "No," she said. "I didn't help them. I only . . . I only . . . closed their eyes. Because they were dead."

The Major stood up again but his place was immediately taken by Sergeant Van Wyk. "We are not talking about that," he snapped. "We are talking about the other help you gave them." Mrs. Allen looked helplessly at the Superintendent and then at the policeman who was taking notes and then at the friendly sergeant.

"Come now, Mrs. Allen; you have nothing to be afraid of. If you have been silly enough to help the terrorists, not because you approve of them, but out of some misguided feelings of humanism," he said gently, "it would be best to tell us now." Then he leaned forward and whispered confidentially in her ear, "It's all right now," he said. "While I'm here you'll be all right; but if you were alone with Sergeant Van Wyk, then there is no telling what he wouldn't do to get the truth from you."

"I protest, Major," said Sergeant Van Wyk. "Sergeant Van der Post has no right to whisper in the accused's ear like that—he is trying to help her; he is not being objective."

Mrs. Allen did not hear what the Major replied, nor what her friendly sergeant said, nor Sergeant Van Wyk's retort; all her attention was fixed on the one word, the "accused"; that was what Sergeant Van Wyk had said—she was sure that was what she had heard. Accused! The accused! What was she accused of? She looked frantically at the four men in the room. Were they really there? Wasn't she perhaps dreaming all this? Wasn't all this part of her not being well? She hadn't been well recently, she knew that; but was this a dream? Was it another of the terrible dreams? She sought frantically for Terry's voice in the empty house of her mind; he wasn't there, there wasn't anybody there, only herself, and she was dreaming all this. It was because of what she had done that afternoon: that was it—it was the feel of cold dead flesh under her fingertips from this afternoon that was making her dream this; in a moment these men would lie down on the floor of the room and would grow dark and dusty and bloody as those other men had been, and she would see their dead eyes again, watching her. It was a dream; if she could just last through a few moments, she would wake up; and the room would be empty again, but she would recognize the place as familiar. She closed her eyes and held hard to the arms of her upright chair.

The friendly sergeant touched her on the shoulder. "Mrs. Allen," he said: "Mrs. Allen. Pay attention to what the Major is saying." She opened her eyes and looked across the desk at him. No, this was not one of the faces from the dream. She watched his mouth as it moved but she could hear no words. What was he saying? She leaned forward and stared at his mouth; it was moving, she could see that, but there was no noise. She shook her head. Now Sergeant Van Wyk crouched down next to her chair; he stared at her and, when she shook her head again, he reached out, almost tenderly, with his hand open so that she could see the circles and valleys of his palm, away from her then and suddenly slapped her with his open palm, hard across her cheek and mouth.

Afterwards, when she was well again, she could remember little of what happened. She remembered answering more questions, she remembered the strange light of the Superintendent's lamp on the desk, she remembered the curled wood of the arms of her chair, she remembered the smell of dust and the Superintendent's cheap tobacco, she remembered the small taste of blood where the sergeant's gold ring had cut her mouth; and then there had been the Major, and he had showed her a bandage, a dirty blood-stained bandage, and he had asked her if she could identify it, and she had shaken her head, and the friendly sergeant had pointed out the initials "SJS" neatly stitched on the bandage, and she had recognized it as one of the bandages from the hospital, and had said so. Then the Major had asked her who had access to the cupboard, who had sewn the initials on to the bandage, whether she had noticed any losses from the bandages recently, or whether they kept a careful inventory. She had answered each question carefully, even though she was weeping most of the time; a little later they had made her take them to the hospital to look at the dispensary. They checked her inventory and the list that she and Dr. Redman kept so carefully; she explained that only she and Dr. Redman had keys; she heard the Major send the Superintendent and Sergeant Van Wyk off to find Dr. Redman; she heard the police question Sister Mbele, who was on duty that night; she heard the Superintendent return to say that Dr. Redman wasn't in his house, although his car was still in the garage; she heard him say that the sergeant was looking throughout the camp for him; she heard the Major use the hospital phone, and heard him instruct the police-station to put road-blocks out for Dr. Redman; and at last she heard the Major telling her, through the blur of exhaustion, doubt, and emptiness, that she might go back to her house if she wished.

Two hours later, when she was asleep and dreaming, as she had thought she had been dreaming earlier, of the four policemen dead on the floor of the Superintendent's room, of the way their dead eyes stared at the strange encircling light of the room, of her bandaged hands that she could not bring near their faces, Dr. Redman came to her house. He tapped at the window till she woke and then whispered to her, through the slightly open window, to let him in, quickly, at the back door. "Quickly, quickly," he urged her; and she, still in her dream, fumbled at the lock, and let him in to the small kitchen. He stepped quickly inside the door, and behind it, pushing it closed as he did so.

"Turn out the light," he said.

Mrs. Allen shook her head. They looked at each other across the room for what must have been a minute before she spoke.

"The police are looking for you."

"I know. Why do you think I look like this?" He gestured at his clothes; they were stained with dust, his face and hands were dirty, his shoes scuffed and grey.

"Where have you been?"

"Hiding up at the cemetery."

"Have the policemen gone?"

"Some of them; they left one man behind. He's watching my house and the hospital in case I come back."

Again there was silence between them; they stood, immobile, looking at each other across the room.

"Did the policeman see you come here?"

Now for the first time he sneered at her; he was himself again. "Are you hoping that he did? That would make it easier for you, wouldn't it?"

"What do you mean?"

"You know bloody well what I mean." He started to move across the room to her, threatening her; but she did not move, so he stopped. "You informed the police, didn't you? You told them about me and Nurse Peters." Slowly Mrs. Allen looked up at him and slowly shook her head; Dr. Redman took another two paces towards her—very quietly he said. "Why bother to lie—you told them, didn't you? Or you told the Superintendent? That's what you did, of course; you told him and then he phoned the police and they came to him and then they called you and you repeated to the police what you had told the Superintendent." Again, Mrs. Allen shook her head slowly.

"Dammit, stop lying," he cried, and then looked round, fearful that the loudness with which he had spoken might have summoned the waiting policeman; there was something like desperation in his voice, as if he had to believe that she had called the police. Once again, they looked at each other and again Mrs. Allen shook her head; then she spoke, in such quiet tones and from so far away that Redman had to strain to hear.

"No," she said. "No, I didn't phone the police, Doctor."

"The hell you didn't," he said fiercely. "Why are they looking for me, then?"

"I didn't tell the police," she said again.

"Look, Mrs. Allen," he said, "I know that you are upset. I know that you think I don't understand, but I do. Please, you must tell the truth—you did tell the police about me and Nurse Peters . . . oh, all right, about me and Nurse Peters and the other nurses."

"It was that, wasn't it?" she said.

"Dammit, what does it matter now? Really, does it matter?" He threw his arms into the air in a gesture of impatience, and half-turned away. "Yes, it's true—it wasn't only Nurse Peters, it was others as well: before, during and after. Do you want names? Details? Do you want me to go to get one of them and show you what I did with them? They would, you know—they loved it, they loved every minute of it. Sometimes I thought that they wanted it more than I did . . ."

Mrs. Allen's hands were over her ears, her eyes closed, her

head turned down to the floor; "Please stop, please stop, please stop," she said again and again, so that her own voice might drown what she heard.

"All right, I'll stop," he said, and repeated, "All right, I'll stop," and when she went on with the monotonous "Please stop," he stepped forward and shook her until she stopped.

"Please, Mrs. Allen, you must answer; you told them, didn't you?"

"No."

"Then why are they looking for me?" he shouted at her, desperately.

As though she had suddenly had a vision, as if the one name of the one god had suddenly been revealed to her, she looked up and said, ludicrously almost, the word so denied the visionary appearance, "Bandages!"

"What do you mean?" Dr. Redman asked. But you do know, she thought, you do know—they were right, the police were right. You're the one, she thought; and although she had been aware of the possibility, even the probability, before then, now she was certain; and horrified at the certainty.

"You know—you do know. One of those dead men, the men who killed the Van Bredas and the policemen . . . he was bandaged; and they said it looked professional. It was you, wasn't it? You took the bandages from the dispensary and you bandaged him . . ." Her voice disappeared; she was looking at a man whom she might never have seen before; oh, it wasn't that the way he looked changed—but it was the way she looked at him. In a way, she knew that she could understand the other business; it was wrong, of course it was wrong, but it was within her range of experience. You knew what the mis-use of the gestures of love was because you knew what real love was; but this . . . this was murder; or it was at least helping men who had most foully murdered very ordinary people, a farmer, his wife, and their children—and policemen, all or most of whom must have had wives and children too. "How could you?" she burst out. "How could you help those men?"

He looked very tired. "Oh," he said, half-sighing, "how do I know. At first I said no; and then I went. You should understand," he added, snorting with what might have turned into laughter at another time. "After all, you helped them too."

"What do you mean?"

"Come on; you closed their eyes—we all saw what you did. It was very brave."

"It wasn't brave," she said passionately. "It was just . . . just what any person would have done, any person who wasn't afraid of the police. It didn't mean that I approve of what they had done—because I don't. They were dead, that was all. What they did was wrong, was terrible—evil!"

"What else could they do?" he said listlessly, not looking at her, looking rather at the locked door.

"There is never an excuse for wrong-doing," she said.

"Isn't there?" he said, not meaning to ask a question; so when she began to reply, he interrupted her. "Oh, for God's sake, this isn't the time for political arguments. Look, please, can we forget all about what was right and what was wrong for a moment, and can you just try to remember what the police said? Please!"

Obstinately, refusing to abandon what little sense of righteousness she had left, Mrs. Allen said, "Right and wrong aren't anything to do with politics."

"Please, Mrs. Allen. Please, I said."

"Oh, I can't remember. It was all like a dream. It was terrible. They said that I must have done it."

"Done what?"

"Oh, you know; helped those men. They said that I had given them the bandages. But all the time it wasn't me, it was you." Very slowly she was moving away from him, moving back against the far wall of the kitchen; she stared at him in horror. "You helped them, and they are murderers. You are a murderer yourself. How . . . how could you?"

"All I did was to help one wounded man—I did what a doctor is supposed to do," he shrugged; he knew, and Mrs. Allen knew, that what he was saying was not true—he had helped them, not as a doctor at all, but simply because that was the only skill which he had to offer them. "What else could I do?" He shrugged again.

"You should not have helped them," Mrs. Allen cried out; she had long since passed any stage of thought—all that was left was the simplified structure of morality that forced her to say that someone else's actions were right or were wrong. She did not want to know why he had helped the terrorists; all that mattered was that he had helped people who had killed other people. "It was wrong to help them, you should not have done it, it was wrong."

Repeating the gesture that Mrs. Allen had made earlier on, he brought his hands up and covered his ears, saying as he did so, "God, will you stop it, Mrs. Allen? Please stop, please stop," repeating this again and again until he realized that she had stopped, that she was watching him again. But he kept his ears covered so that when she spoke he had to ask her, "What did you say?"

"I said, What are you going to do now?"

He shrugged again. "Wait, I suppose. Wait until they find me."

"Can't you get away?" She knew that she was talking now against what Terry would have said—he had always believed, he had always told the children that, no matter what wrong you had done, it was never sensible to run away but always wise to stay and face the consequences. You had to stay to fight things out, to see things through to an end. "Can't you," she asked again, "Can't you get away across the border?"

"What's the point?" he said. "Really, what is the point of doing that?"

"But if they catch you they'll hang you."

He nodded. "Probably," he said, and smiled strangely. "They won't like it that a white man helped the . . . what shall we call them, Mrs. Allen? . . . murderers? Terrorists? Freedom-fighters? Liberators?"

"You don't free anybody by killing."

"I think you do," he said. He seemed now to have found himself again, to be as cocky and confident as always. He tilted his head sideways and tipped his chin. "If we had done a bit more killing before, we wouldn't be in this mess."

"If we had done less, we mightn't be either," Mrs. Allen said obstinately, and was going to say more but his face prevented her. It was a terrible face, she thought, like the face he had in her dreams, a confident look on the surface, yes, but a face almost without features in the hard light, the face he had had when he told her what he would do to himself if she went to the police. He would do it, she knew; there was no need for the voices to keep repeating that. That was what he was planning; that was why he was smiling that strange half-smile; that was why she was smiling back at him, the same strange half-smile that bore as little relation to a smile as old Joseph's cackle did to laughter. Where was Terry's voice, she wondered, but without any real concern; what could he say now, even if he knew what she knew?

He was still watching her, this man whose face she had dreamt, and he was saying something to her.

"What did you say?" she asked, drawing her own voice back from the crowd that flocked and jostled and whispered.

"I said, Will you do something for me? Will you?" he asked, and he smiled again.

"All right," he said, when she did not answer, "I'll tell you what before, before I ask you. Will you let me have your keys to the dispensary? Mine are in my house and I can't go there."

"Why do you want them?"

"I've got some things in the hospital that I want to collect. They'll help me get away." Seeing that she hesitated, he went on, "Money. That's what I've got there. I keep some money in my desk. I'll need it."

"That's not true. I know what you want—you want something else. You want . . . you want . . ." She knew what he wanted; and she would not say it, she could not say it.

"Give me your keys," he said.

Without speaking, she shook her head slowly.

"Then I shall have to take them." He moved slowly towards her and, as slowly, she moved along the wall away from him. Then she could not help herself, she had to look; the keys were usually kept hanging on a hook just inside the door of the kitchen. He saw her look and looked himself. They were there, hanging on a hook inside the door. Quite casually, he walked across the room and took them; while Mrs. Allen stood still, watching him, doing nothing, saying nothing, not even "No. No. No." As he opened the door, he turned back to her and, still with the strange little smile, said, "If you follow me, I shall kill you. Go back to bed now and forget; go back to your dreams, Mrs. Allen." Then he was out of the door and she could hear the first few steps he took over the hard-packed dust outside her door.

How long she stood there she could not afterwards remember. Staring at the closed door, listening to the silence that invaded the small noise his shoes had made on the path, she waited; all the rooms of the house were empty, the voices gone, and she walked slowly from room to room, not caring that there was no one speaking. Suddenly there was shouting—where did it come from, she thought; from my head, from outside? What was the shouting? What was the point of shouting? Everything had been decided. She knew exactly what was happening. She understood it all. There was no puzzle about anything any more. It had happened, that was all.

"Help, help," the voices outside cried; Mrs. Allen walked slowly to the door and turned off the lights. "Help, help," the voices cried. Slowly Mrs. Allen walked across the kitchen and back to her bedroom. "Help, help," the voices cried.

*   *   *

They found Dr. Redman's body in the fields to the west of the settlement next morning. It was simple to reconstruct what had happened. With the keys that he had forced Mrs. Allen to give him, he had gone straight to the hospital, chancing the fact that the policeman might have been there; he wasn't—he had decided it was more important to watch Dr. Redman's house, since that was where he would need to go if he wanted to have a chance of escaping—his car was there, his money was there; they had found it when they searched. Dr. Redman had walked into the hospital, had walked quietly past the nurses' room, where Sister Mbele had been asleep, and had gone to the surgery. One of the patients had been awake, however, and seeing him had crept out of bed to summon Sister Mbele. She had gone to the dispensary where she had found Dr. Redman, busy taking something from the dispensing cupboard. She had asked him what he was doing and he had, "like someone who was mad", she told the policeman who took her statement, attacked her—she had gone running out into the dust-bowl calling for help and the policeman had come running. Together they had rushed back to the hospital, and had got to the dispensary just in time to see Dr. Redman climbing out of a window. The policeman had fired a shot at him but had missed and had fired again twice into the darkness as Dr. Redman ran away but had missed again. He had, later, phoned for reinforcements but in the black Transvaal night there had been little hope of finding him; not that the police cared much, anyway; they knew that they would be able to get him in the daylight. A white man wouldn't be able to move far in that countryside without being spotted.

Next to his body in the fields they had found a syringe and eighteen empty capsules marked Morphia. Dr. Redman, meticulous doctor that he was, had injected enough into his thigh to kill himself twice over; for ten minutes he must have sat there, gradually getting drowsy until he went into coma. Within half an hour, before the police reinforcements arrived even, he had died of respiratory failure—even if they had found him before he went into coma, they could not have saved him.

Mrs. Allen, still in her nightdress and dressing-gown, watched the police carry his body in to the settlement. It isn't surprising really, she thought, as she wandered through the empty rooms of her house; there was nothing that I could do about it. He needed to do that; what else could he have done? She looked through the rooms to see if there was anyone there who could answer the question; but there was nobody; so what point was there in worrying? And then she heard the terrible and single voice, falling down on her body like a vulture, then disembodied, then coming up from behind the house, laughing, cackling, laughing, getting louder and louder, laughing, louder and louder, until the voice entered the house and began to fill every room with the single noise, while she, in terror, fled through the empty rooms looking for Terry, searching for him to stand against this terrible voice that she thought had gone away, and when she didn't find him, searching for somewhere, anywhere, to hide; but it was no good, there was only the one voice, and every moment it grew louder and it grew louder until the whole world was contained in the sound.

* * *

Simbele, watching from the open window of the classroom,

saw the procession down from the fields, the six policemen, two of them carrying the stretcher on which Redman's body lay. Petrus had told him that they were searching for Redman; everyone in the camp knew by morning that he had attacked Sister Mbele and had escaped despite the policeman's shooting. Simbele himself had heard the shots, had woken, had gone to the window of his room, and had seen nothing.

Well, he thought, there was another: so now he shared in another; and what could he do but go on? There would be an end to it, sooner or later, for him at least; he'd see the last of them, perhaps, or perhaps he would grow not to care. Would that be the way to go, the way of not caring? Or the way of this man whom the police were carrying carefully down through the fields to the police van? Quietly like that, simply like that; choosing your own time, your own place? Or perhaps he might have time to go out, across the fields and the ridges of dried earth, to the mountains, to wherever the others had moved to, and there die the longer way, but easy enough too, in the end. He tried to remember what it had been that Dr. Redman had said to him on their way back from tending Moshi's brother— he seemed to remember that it had been something about not being afraid. He had not answered, had not even listened, because there were other things that mattered more than why one white man should risk so much for people who were not his own. Perhaps he had decided to die because he was afraid of telling the police what he knew, afraid of naming Simbele, afraid of walking back across the valley in the darkness to lead the police to the gorge and then up to the cave, where there would be nobody now. Or perhaps he had decided even then, when he had been looking at that mutilated head, and cleaning it, and covering it up again decently with those bandages. Perhaps he had wanted this, so that it was not an escape, but the only road, the all-road to the same place as all roads. But it was too late to wonder now; the man had chosen and there was the procession, coming down the hill with his body, and he would tell nobody now.

He saw, across the dust-bowl, Mrs. Allen standing in her dressing-gown in the doorway of her house, watching the procession as it came into the dust-bowl. What did she feel, he wondered. And there, he noted, was old Joseph, come from the cemetery, still carrying his spade, almost running with an old man's shuffling steps, anxious to see the dead man, anxious to measure him with his practised eye—and laughing his senile laugh, that did as well as weeping in that place. Well, there would be two or three who wept for this one, he thought. And perhaps that was enough to want. . . .

A noise from the classroom drew his attention back from his own mind; some of the children had clambered on their desks to watch the procession. He turned away from the window and back into the room, ordered the children to get on with their work, and went back to his seat and his own work. There was no one weeping here, he thought, not even Petrus, with his careful face and steady hand; it was just another white man dead.

PART THREE

Immortality

XI

When Mrs. Allen came back to the settlement, two months later, she was better again; or that was what the doctor said. They had said that before she was released from the hospital which she had been sent to by her daughter and son-in-law; it hadn't been a serious breakdown, they said—she had been under intolerable pressure, of course, they said, but removed from the isolation of the settlement, the attention of the police, and the difficulty of events, she would be able to come to terms with her husband's death more adequately. In many ways, it was the outside world, not the one inside her mind, that made her collapse; they said. A month at the hospital was more than enough; indeed, if her son-in-law hadn't been in the profession himself, they would probably have sent her away as stable within two weeks. Again, she had made herself useful; as one of the doctors said to her son-in-law, they would have liked to keep her there indefinitely, she had made herself so competently useful during her breakdown; but that wouldn't be fair, he said too—she was well, and what she needed most was to get back into normal living patterns, whatever those were, as soon as possible.

So, when Mrs. Allen told Caroline and Charles that she had booked herself on the train in a week's time to return to the settlement and Verderdorp, they were both flabbergasted; for a time Charles, thinking more as her daughter's husband than as a psychiatrist, even thought of trying to persuade the hospital to take her back again; but he knew there was little point, for it was clear that she was completely all right—why, she was even capable of talking about her breakdown in open and honest terms—she had been ill, she knew that she had been ill, and, as Charles always said, an illness of the mind was just another version of an illness of the body; and the first stage of recuperation was to acknowledge that you had been ill.

Peter had cabled the moment he heard of the breakdown, asking if he should fly out. "Typical," said Caroline to her husband; "I do love Peter but really it's typical—he hasn't written to Mother for months, and now he cables to ask if he should come out. If you were Peter, you would have flown out here without asking." Charles, flattered that his wife always had such a high opinion of him, still did not want to get involved in family squabbles, even on his wife's side; he adored Caroline, she was a splendid wife and mother, utterly loyal and very sensible, but the Allen family as a whole—the dead as well as the living—was something of a mystery to him, with their certainties, their ancestral sensibilities, their disapproval of anyone who tried, as he tried, to see the full complexities, both psychological and material, of any situation. But he drafted a cable in reply to Peter's and signed it, "Caroline and Charles"—SUGGEST YOUR COMING UNNECESSARY STOP MOTHER NOT SERIOUSLY ILL STOP SHE NEEDS COMPLETE REST, it read—and he helped Caroline compose a letter to Peter which suggested, very tactfully of course, that he help pay part of his mother's fare for a long holiday in England when she recovered enough to travel. "After all," Caroline said to Charles, "he's earning a ruddy great fortune there, more than you earn, and it isn't as though he's got children."

But when Peter wrote to his mother, offering to pay her fare to England if she cared to come for a holiday when she was well again, Mrs. Allen replied that though she would love to come, for the time being she couldn't, as really she had to get back to the settlement as soon as possible. That evening, she took Peter's letter and her reply in to Caroline as she sat with Charles in the living-room, and made her read them both. "You see," she said, "I really am going back to the settlement—though it was kind of you to suggest to Peter that he invite me to England," and, when Caroline protested feebly that she hadn't done anything of the kind, she answered firmly, "Now Caroline, I know both you and Peter too well to believe that."

Try as they might, they could not persuade her to give up her plans for returning. "You see," Mrs. Allen explained, partly to herself, "Now that I know just what may happen, now that I understand just what the pressures are, I'll be able to cope with them very easily. My breakdown was the result of special circumstances; the circumstances have changed, and even if they hadn't, I would still know how to deal with them. You see, it's really very simple; it's nothing to do with what happens inside my mind—the doctors told me that—and now that I know that, nothing that happens outside will affect me." Caroline was not convinced, though not for the same reasons as her husband; she was not sure that she trusted psychiatry, with its division of the world into two kinds, the kind inside and the kind outside; though of course she never said so, for it would have hurt her husband, and her father had always taught her to think that not hurting people was the same as loyalty, and loyalty was more important than honesty. There were many things about her father and mother that she no longer accepted; but that at least she knew would never change. So she could not really say what she felt to her mother, in case her mother interpreted it as disloyalty to Peter. So, despite their worry about Mrs. Allen's plans, they gradually came round to the view that it might be all right for her to return.

Then they changed their minds again, because they read a report in the main Sunday newspaper the week before Mrs. Allen was due to return.

EMERGENCY IN TSWANALAND, the headline said. TERRORISTS KILL THREE FAMILIES. CONVICTS JOIN ESCAPE.

"Following three separate but apparently connected attacks by terrorists on farming families in the region of Verderdorp and Grysberg in Tswanaland during the past week, the Minister of Justice has declared a state of emergency in the area.

"Details of the attacks are not very clear, since the police refuse to give any information to the press. However, according to reliable local information, the farmers attacked by the terrorists are the Viljoens, the Van Rensburgs and the Rees family. It is thought that the attacks took place last Wednesday night.

"There has been intense police and army activity in the region ever since. The local police of Verderdorp are confident that they will corner the terrorists soon.

"Information has also been received from a fairly reliable source that convicts working for one of the murdered farmers, Mr. Viljoen of Spiesvlei, were released by the terrorists. Some of these joined the terrorists and those who refused were brutally shot down. Most of the convicts would have been short-term prisoners, since it is the stated policy of the Department of Prisons not to use long-term prisoners for farm-labour."

The rest of the article contained information relating to the previous terrorist activity in the region and details of just what a regional state of emergency meant.

Mrs. Allen, looking at the newspaper while she lay in bed—for every morning her daughter, once she had got her children off to school and her husband to his consulting rooms, brought her a tray and the newspaper to her bedroom, before going back downstairs to give her maid instructions for the day—read the report with the interest not of someone involved but with the interest of the ordinary citizen; the room in which she lay was sunny, the wall-paper was pleasantly green, the furniture was spotless and the noises downstairs comforting, the hoover in the children's playroom, the banging of pots being washed in the kitchen, the gardener whistling as he weeded the long lawn that ran down to the blue-tiled swimming-bath. It was bound to be difficult, she thought, to feel all that much concerned, even though she thought she remembered meeting the Viljoens once, when they stopped at the settlement on the way to Verderdorp. How could one connect that world of dust and blood in the dust with this one of green lawns and blue swimming-baths? She knew that there were connections; she knew that if she went downstairs to talk to the maid—if a black woman would talk to a white about such things—she would discover that, say, her husband was in gaol for a pass offence, her brother had fled the country, and her children were not in school for longer than two years at the average; her house, too, was probably not much better than the huts on the settlement. But lying there, in this comfortable room in this wealthy suburb, it was easy not to remember. The newspapers could talk about what happened in Tswanaland, in the Transkei, on the borders of Moçambique, in Rhodesia, but lying here you had only your memory—which was untrustworthy in many things—and your imagination—which was best kept under firm control these days. They could tell you the most terrible things, if you listened to what they said; but your senses denied what they said, your senses said only, We do not recognize these things of which you talk; we recognize only the pleasant colours and the comforting sounds.

Having noted all this, Mrs. Allen, being Mrs. Allen, immediately got up, bathed, dressed, and went downstairs, where she spent the morning doing the darning and mending that her daughter had "not been able to get round to" for the past six weeks. In the afternoon she slept for a time, went out then to post a letter and, later, when the children came back from nursery school, took them for a walk to the park half a mile away. At dinner that evening, when her son-in-law said, "Did you see the papers this morning, Mrs. Allen?"—he was a formal young man, pompous even, and he always called her

Mrs. Allen, not Mary as she had suggested he do—and when he exchanged a quick glance with Caroline, she knew that they had discussed the reports and were hoping to persuade her that it would be physically dangerous for her to return to the settlement.

"Yes," Mrs. Allen said evenly. "It is horrible, isn't it. I expect it is the same terrorists who were operating there before; they probably went away over the border and then came in again. I think that I must have met the Viljoens."

"Who?" asked her daughter.

"The Viljoens. They were one of the families that were killed."

Caroline put down her knife and fork and said, firmly, "Well, Mommy, I hope that at least persuades you how ridiculous your plan of returning to St Joseph's is."

"Why?" said Mrs. Allen.

"Good heavens, Mrs. Allen," Charles answered. "It's pretty obvious. It's only a matter of time before there is either a full-scale rebellion in the region or the police start reprisals—and since they already suspect you of being involved with the terrorists, you are not likely to be left alone."

"Come, Charles," said Mrs. Allen, smiling. "For an intelligent man as you are supposed to be, you don't argue very well. The terrorists are hardly likely to attack the settlement; it may not be much of a place, but at least there are black people there as well as white—the terrorists won't want to kill their own people..."

"That's not true," Peter interrupted. "Look what the paper said about the convicts they killed for refusing to join them. They obviously don't have a scruple in the world—white people, black people, it's all the same to them. They won't stop to ask you, 'What are your politics, dear lady?' They'll kill first and ask questions afterwards—if they don't do other things as well."

"Don't be disgusting, Charles," said Caroline. "There is no need to lay on details with a trowel." She turned to her mother. "You see, however, Mommy, that your returning is quite out of the question. If you really feel that you must have a job, you can always get one around here—Charles could probably find a decent job for you at one of the hospitals, if you want to go on with that sort of work."

"I already have a perfectly good job, Caroline," said Mrs. Allen, "I am still being paid by the Church, remember, even though I am on sick leave. The Bishop himself told me that there was no question of their replacing me. I am going back—and that's all there is to say." She pushed her chair an inch or two back from the table and leaned forward, smiling. "Besides, I've booked a seat on the train to Verderdorp on Friday. I phoned this morning. So I shall be back there by Saturday afternoon—I've written to the Superintendent to ask him to meet me. That's really all there is to say on the subject. Shall we talk about something else?"

Though they did not talk about anything else, though the argument ended with Caroline in tears and Charles furious, threatening to get his colleagues to certify that Mrs. Allen was dangerously ill and should be committed to hospital again, nevertheless she won, at least in the sense that she went back to the settlement when she had planned. The only change in her plans was that Caroline drove her back to the settlement and of course argued with her the whole way; at first it was going to be Charles, or that was what Caroline had suggested, two nights after the final row about her mother's return. "At least you must let Charles drive you to Verderdorp," she had said. Charles had looked very worried and had said, "You know that I can't do it this next weekend, Caroline—there's the conference." The "conference" was one on the psychological effects of migrant labour to which Charles was delivering a paper embodying some research he had done on the problem in a local

African township. So Caroline said that she would drive her mother down herself—she would only be away one night and Charles would be back then; during the day the black nanny could look after the children. So Mrs. Allen, after arguing half-heartedly that Caroline should not trouble herself and should not neglect the children for her sake, agreed; telling the truth to herself, she knew that the prospect of the train journey appalled her—all that heat and dust, all that dirt. For even though you had those things, heat, dust, dirt and worse, at the settlement, you had there, some of the time, a sense of service, a sense of sacrifice for an ideal. That was what Terry had always said was the most important thing in anyone's life—the sense of serving some power greater than yourself, whether it was God or an ideal or a theory. What was wrong with this life in the rich suburbs of Johannesburg, wasn't the comfort, the green and controlled lawns and the tidy blue swimming bath, the good sense of the servants accustomed to their mistress's wishes and the sensible shops half a mile down the road—no, those things were marvellous, provided that they went with the sense of service; and she knew that she would not be able to find that here.

All the same, it was not simply the thought of the train journey that appalled her; she was too aware still of the chaos in her own mind to look forward to her return without a sense of foreboding. The doctors had told her that she should feel no guilt about Redman; they had persuaded her to tell them every-thing—and they put everything in such clinical terms that some-how everything seemed devoid of morality. There had been morality involved—she knew that perfectly well, though she had not said that to the doctors—but those last few weeks had been so tormented that she could not remember the details; she had a vague sense of having made mistakes, but the sense was overpowered by the memory of fear and by the imagined consequences. The sorting out had still to come; but nothing could be sorted out here—besides, the Bishop had written to say how much he hoped that she would return to continue her good work at the settlement. He did not think that he would be able to find anyone else prepared to take on the work, he said quite openly, in his letters, and he was also afraid that there would be no replacement for the unfortunate Dr. Redman. Sister Mbele, he wrote, had been doing valiantly in the absence of a doctor and a matron—the Bishop had not been to the settlement himself, but he had sent his archdeacon to investigate the situation and had had from him a long letter which he referred to occasionally in his letter to Mrs. Allen. But even Sister Mbele had not the ability to cope on her own, especially as they had lost one of the nurses, who had, without warning, run off to Johannesburg. Reading that letter, Mrs. Allen knew that she was right to go back; she must go back, really she must, she said to herself. There was no guarantee that she would not be ill again, but she resolved that at least she would make an effort this time not to isolate herself as completely as she had done before her illness—she would not limit herself solely to the settlement but would try to make friends outside: she would get in touch with the small Anglican community in Verderdorp, she would accept offers of lifts to the town whenever they were made, she would read the newspapers every day even though they might be three days' old when she got them, she would listen religiously—in the sense of observance, not belief —to the national and local news every morning, she would write even more often to the children and to her old friends and would hope to hear often from them. That might help her keep a perspective on events if ever they became terrible again —and you had to expect that they would, she said to herself, because you had already had your warning.

But as far as going back was concerned, she had no choice, really; "What else can I do?" she used to say aloud when she was on her own—she did not remember that was the phrase Dr.

Redman had used. She remembered some things, but not many, from those last forty-eight hours—she remembered the police, she remembered Dr. Redman coming to get the keys, she remembered seeing them bringing his body in from the fields, and then there were long blanks, out of which appeared sudden images—of sun streaming through dust, of her own hands that seemed to grow enormous as she watched them, of children laughing, and, strangest of all, Simbele talking very gently to her, as he might have done to one of his pupils. But it had the illogicality of a dream remembered, full of transitions that must have seemed logical at the time but which now seemed ludicrous. Well, it didn't really matter, she thought; she could ask somebody when she got back there. She was almost all right now; she'd manage somehow.

So, early that Saturday morning, Caroline drove her mother down to the settlement, through the plains of the highveld, down through the escarpment, and then up into the semi-desert of Tswanaland. The only major delay on the journey was caused by a police check on the road between Verderdorp and the settlement—two white women travelling alone worried the police first for one reason and then, after Mrs. Allen had been, as her daughter put it afterwards, "appallingly, unnecessarily rude" to them, for another, and so their car was searched for nearly an hour. But by five they were at the settlement. At six Caroline left again for Johannesburg—she was going to stop for the night at a motel, and then press on early next morning, so that she would be back home for lunch. Mrs. Allen tried to persuade her to stay over at the settlement for a night, but Caroline (partly because she wanted to show her mother that she still disapproved) insisted on going back almost immediately; all that she consented to do was to visit Dr. Allen's grave and to look at the hospital buildings. She wasn't really interested, Mrs. Allen could sense—and she could understand that too, for she knew that her daughter had committed herself not to the ideals which she and Terry had always served, but to the ideal of being a mother and a wife, a home-body rather than a help-meet, as her mother had been. Well, thought Mrs. Allen, that was one way of behaving—it wouldn't have done for her, it wouldn't do for her now. She and Terry had served some power greater than themselves, and she would go on serving that power, even if the service broke her.

When Caroline had gone, Mrs. Allen went back to the cemetery; old Joseph was nowhere to be seen and so she could do what she needed to, which was to stand there among the long shadows of the gravestones and the wooden crosses, her own shadow stretching enormously, and let the voices return to the empty house; without thinking she spoke aloud to Terry, listening carefully all the time for his voice among the other voices—he would come back now, she was sure, because he had never really gone away. He had stayed here, waiting for her among the graves.

When she had finished, she turned back down the hill and walked carefully along the winding goat-path that led to the settlement. She went first to the hospital, where she had a long discussion with Sister Mbele about everything that had to be done the next day. Later she walked through the dust to Simbele's cottage, knocked at the door, and, when he appeared, said to him, "I can't remember exactly what happened that last day I was here. But I seem to remember that you were kind to me, and so I am coming to thank you." Not waiting for a reply, she turned away immediately and walked back across the dust-bowl towards the Superintendent's house; she hadn't, deliberately, called on Mr. Schwartz when she arrived—there were other more important things to do—but she knew that eventually she must see him, whatever his reaction to her was going to be now. He had been horrible to her when the police were trying to find out about the bandages; but that wasn't really his fault—he was on the same side as the police automatically; his upbringing had conditioned him to that sort of response and you couldn't really blame a man for what his people had done to him, she thought. He had however been remarkably sensible about her illness; he had phoned her daughter in Johannesburg and had arranged for an ambulance to drive her there, direct to the hospital which her son-in-law had suggested; he had informed the Bishop by telegram; he had got Sister Mbele to pack a suitcase of clothes for her; and he had phoned a doctor in Verderdorp to come out to give her heavy sedation. She hadn't known any of this, of course; all the time she was waiting for the ambulance to arrive, she had sat in her own sitting-room, watched over first by Simbele and then by Sister Mbele, with her hands over her face and weeping, weeping, weeping, without end. Now, walking through the dust towards the Superintendent's house, Mrs. Allen tried as hard as she could to remember what exactly she had done—she could remember thinking that she might be going mad, but the actual time of madness, from the moment she had seen the police carrying Dr. Redman's body down from the fields and across the dust-bowl to the hospital, to her waking in the clean green-and-white rooms of the Johannesburg hospital, were almost entirely blank—there were flashes of memory, but little more: she knew that Simbele had been kind to her, that Sister Mbele had been kind; the rest of the details she had gathered together from what the doctors told her, from what her daughter told her, and from what little she remembered. It didn't matter, really, she hadn't been herself, and now she was herself again.

She knew that, to an outsider, her coming back might perhaps seem strange; but how could you explain, she wondered, even to your son or daughter. How could anyone who didn't exist inside you as well as outside you, as Terry had done, possibly understand, even if you explained carefully. Why, they probably couldn't understand even why you had come here in the first place—Peter hadn't understood, Caroline had only partly understood—and so how could they possibly understand why you came back again? For Mrs. Allen knew that the feelings that had brought her to the settlement for the first time were much the same as those that brought her there again, after her illness; you made up your mind to do something, she thought, and you did it. It was just the same way that some plants grew; you put them into the right kind of soil, and there was almost nothing you could do to stop them growing after that. You could chop them down; but their roots would survive and they would flower again—you could drop a great rock on top of them; but they would grow round the rock and up to the light—you could dig them up and throw them on to a rubbish dump; but they would root themselves even there and would flower again. For her, there was no stopping now; you just had to go on, she thought—you didn't know exactly why, but you went on and you made yourself useful, you worked, because living meant working. Of course, the dreams were still there; they were always there, and there was no longer any point in whispering them aloud when you woke from them in the morning. But they were dreams and as long as you kept them separate you could manage; the night-time was for the dreams, yes, but the day-time . . . the day-time was for other things, among which were the voices, yes, but other things too. You just had to shut the dreams away, just as you had to shut the voices away, if you wanted to get anything done; you had to pretend that they weren't there, you had to pretend that you were completely well again and then you would be well, whatever the voices said.

XII

Simbele was puzzled by Mrs. Allen's brief visit to thank him; he had known that she was coming back to the settlement—the Superintendent had told Sister Mbele ten days before, Petrus had told him, and the news had spread very quickly. He was not surprised that she had come back; he knew the reasons both instinctively, in such a way that he didn't have to put them into words, but she had also said, in her madness, that she would come back. Last time he had seen her, when he had helped Sister Mbele put her, heavily drugged and weeping, into the ambulance, she had kept on muttering that: "I'll come back to help you, Sister, I'll come back, don't you worry, I'll soon be better again, and then I'll come back." He didn't understand exactly why she had gone mad, but of course, once you knew, you could remember the signs there had been before it, her strange behaviour with the dead terrorists, her ritual afterwards at the place where their bodies had lain, her immobile watching of the procession bringing Redman's body in from the fields.

How strange it had been, he thought, and how strange his own reactions had been. Just as he had thought that one of the reasons that Dr. Redman had killed himself might be his desire to protect Simbele—for Redman had not come near him while the police were searching for him, had not even come to him before going out into the fields—so he had known that he had an obligation to Mrs. Allen mad, that he had not had to her sane. He had heard the children at the back of the class laughing at something and, after giving them a moment or two to settle down on their own, had turned round to tell them to get on with their work—he was teaching arithmetic to the older children at the front of the class. He saw them standing up, some on desks, looking out of the window, laughing and pointing at something out there. He called out, "Sit down, all of you, and get on with your work," but much to his surprise—for the class was usually meticulously obedient, almost too obedient sometimes—they took no notice of what he said, though one or two looked round and thought of obeying, before the something outside caught their attention again and they began to laugh and whisper and point and giggle. Simbele walked quickly to one of the windows himself; and what he saw there made him move quickly down the classroom to the door and out into the dust-bowl.

The something that had so amused the children was Mrs. Allen. Bedraggled, hair unkempt, dress crumpled and dirty, she was walking round and round in the middle of the dust-bowl, in a tight little circle, dragging behind her a bundle of blankets and pillows, tied together with cords and pieces of rope. Every few yards in her endless walking of the circle, she would stop, and look round her anxiously, as if she were looking for something.

Simbele, without pausing to think, ran out into the sunny dust-bowl, calling as he did so, "Mrs. Allen, Mrs. Allen." He heard footsteps in the dust behind him and turned quickly, to see that half the children were following him, still giggling and pointing. "Go back," he cried at them. "Go back to your work." They stopped and he could see that, for once, they were willing to disobey him. "Go back," he cried again, and made a movement towards them with an arm raised, as if he were going to pursue them to strike them. They turned then and began slowly to move back, looking round every few paces to see what he was doing. Simbele moved forward again, more slowly now, and when he was a few yards away from her, called out, "Mrs. Allen," again; she didn't seem to hear him, so he went up close to her. She looked at him, with strange eyes, and said, "Please sir, will you help me? I have found this dead man"—she gestured behind her to the bundle of blankets and pillows—"and I have forgotten where the cemetery is." She reached forward to take him by the upper arm. "Please sir, I must find the cemetery. We must bury him. Will you help me, please?" With her strange eyes she looked at him, as if she had never seen him before, as if she were a child asking the way from a stranger.

"Come, Mrs. Allen," Simbele said. "I'll show you. But first we must take him to the hospital to see if he is really dead." He held out a hand to her and she reached forward and put her hand in his.

"Thank you," she said. "But there's no need to go to the hospital."

"Let me take him for you," said Simbele, putting his other hand on the rope which she had tied to the bundle. Furiously, Mrs. Allen pulled her hand away from his and stepped back a yard or two, so that he could not touch the rope. "No," she said. "You are not allowed to touch him. You are not allowed to; nobody but me is allowed to touch." She smiled suddenly, brilliantly, and then moved forward again to his side. Looking around carefully, she turned back to him, leaned forward and whispered, "You see, somebody else might wake him up. He's not really dead—he's only pretending to be dead. He'll wake up soon—that's why I want to take him to the cemetery. You do understand, don't you?"

"Yes," said Simbele, soothingly. "Yes, I do understand. But we must take him to the hospital first." Somehow he had to get her there—he looked round; a few people were watching from the huts and he could see that children were still standing outside the classroom, too fascinated to go in, and that others were looking from the windows. But there was no sign of any of the nurses and none of the Superintendent. Mrs. Allen had not moved. "Come," Simbele said again and held out his hand to her; once again she took it and he began to lead her back towards the hospital. After they walked a few steps, she began without warning to curse, slow, relished, foul words; and then she began to weep and tried to pull her hand away from Simbele's—he refused to let go and she shook her hand violently, pushed him away with the other, hit him as hard as she could with her free hand, but still he refused to let go. Suddenly, she became completely docile again, and as he led her across the dust-bowl again, she began to chatter as a child might, but talking gibberish.

Well, Simbele remembered, that had been just about all; when he was nearly at the hospital, Sister Mbele had come rushing out with Petrus, who must have seen from the classroom what Simbele was doing and who, sensible as he always was, had known that his mother would be needed. She had helped Simbele lead Mrs. Allen in to the women's ward, had sent Petrus off to get the Superintendent, and had, carefully and kindly, helped to calm Mrs. Allen. The Superintendent had come, had taken one look at Mrs. Allen, had listened impatiently to what Simbele had to say, and had then rushed off to phone for a doctor from the town. He had hardly left when he reappeared again to say, "I think that you should take Mrs. Allen to her own quarters, Sister," and had then scurried off again. So Simbele and Sister Mbele had, between them, led Mrs. Allen back to her cottage and, while Simbele waited in the front room, Sister Mbele had persuaded Mrs. Allen to lie down on her bed.

The doctor had come an hour later and had given her what Sister Mbele told him was a sedative drug, and he had been able to go home. Later that night an ambulance had come and Mrs. Allen had been taken away.

He had known it would not be the last they saw of her, though, in many ways, he wished that it might be. He had not wanted to see her again, he had been quite content to put her out of his mind, for he had been surprised that he had felt such sympathy for her, surprised and a little disturbed. He had not known that a woman like that could feel so deeply. Now that she had come back to the settlement, he would have to think about her again; and he had enough already to think of not to want to have anything else. He admitted to himself, however, that what else he had on his mind at the moment did not really require much thought; he had thought about it before—now he had only to act. Thought these days was really a luxury. So perhaps he was simply afraid to think about Mrs. Allen, to think of what it was that had happened in her mind; because he understood, he knew already.

With the death of Moshi and his brother, he had half-expected that his connection with the terrorists would end; he had been a little surprised when Petrus brought him another message that he should meet them at the High Hill on the far side of the Viljoen farm. He had gone again, taking the last of the tinned food which he kept in a cupboard in his hut. He had met them and had done what they asked him to. Two days later he had woken at midnight to hear the sound of firing from the direction of the Viljoen farm and he had understood why they had asked him to do it. They had asked him to write a letter to the police, warning them that he had heard that there was to be an attack by the terrorists on the police station at Verderdorp that night, and signing himself "A Christian who does not believe in bloodshed." He had printed out one draft of the letter carefully and had copied it again on to a sheet of paper torn from an exercise book in the school cupboard, deliberately making the kind of spelling mistakes that one of his senior pupils would be likely to make. Petrus had borrowed a bicycle and had ridden up to the main road to the only post-box within miles and had posted it.

The day after the attack, when the police were still trying to prevent the escape of the terrorists, now reinforced by the convicts whom they had freed from the compound at the Viljoen farm, Petrus had come to him after class. Standing in front of Simbele's desk, the boy had suddenly begun to cry.

"What is it, Petrus?" Simbele asked.

The boy shook his head and then said, "The man who used to . . . the leader; they killed him last night."

"Who killed him?" asked Simbele softly.

"They say it was the farmer, old Viljoen. But it was not."

"His own men killed him?" Simbele asked, and then he knew.

"It was that one, that one with the scar on his face," and he made the scar on his own face with his finger. The boy nodded, tears streaming down his face.

"How do you know, Petrus?" The boy looked up at him but did not answer. "Why did they do it? Do you know why?"

"It was because he would not let them kill the prisoners." Then, in a rush, the story came out. After they had killed the farmer and his family, they had gone to the compound—the three warders whom the farmer employed to guard the prisoners had run away the moment the attack started so they met no resistance when they broke down the padlocked doors. There were fifteen convicts inside, all dressed in the distinctive red and white uniforms of prison labourers, all thin, half-starved. The leader had asked if any of them wished to join the terrorists and eleven of the fifteen had come forward. Then the man with the scar on his face had stepped forward and raised his automatic rifle to shoot the other four; roughly, the leader had prevented him. For a minute or two the two men had argued there, while the four convicts stood terrified against the back wall of their prison. Then, quite suddenly, the man with the scar had brought his rifle up to the leader's chest and had shot him twice, killing him instantly. Then he had shot the four convicts too.

"And you were there all the time, Petrus?" Simbele asked softly.

"Yes," the boy replied, and fumbled in his pocket; he held his hand forward for Simbele to see what it was he had and

Simbele saw that in his palm there were two shining cartridge cases. Puzzled, he looked up again to Petrus's face and Petrus told him. "It was from these that the bullets that killed the leader came. I picked them up from the floor when no one was looking. One day," he said, "one day . . ."

"You can't keep those," Simbele said flatly. "If the police find them, they will know that you were there. Give them to me," he ordered.

Petrus closed his hand sharply. "No," he said. "I shall keep them safely. You need not worry; nobody will find them. One day . . ." he repeated softly.

"Where have they gone now?" Simbele asked.

The boy gestured with his hand, still looking at the two cartridge cases in his hand. "They are still in the mountains," he said.

"But I thought . . ." Simbele said. "I thought that they had planned to go back . . ." He meant over the border; but faced with this boy who had seen things that no man would see without being shaken to the depth, he knew that he had no need to explain.

"No," said Petrus. "That was the old leader's plan. The new leader thinks that they should stay. I think that is perhaps the other reason he killed him. They are staying, some of them in the mountains. Some have gone to other places." He looked down at the cartridge cases again and then smiled a grown-up's hard smile. "So, one day . . ." he said again, and turned and walked out of the classroom.

Watching the door of the classroom that Petrus had closed so carefully and quietly behind him, Simbele thought again of what the boy must have seen. What had they put into this boy's mind, he wondered; when he had cried in front of his teacher, had he cried for himself? Or had he cried for those four frightened men who waited against the wall, his own people, ordinary in their crimes, ordinary in their fear, ordinary in not choosing, and nothing in death? Or had he cried for the old leader? Yes, thought Simbele, it was probably mostly for the old leader, the man who had made Petrus start on the all-road, for Petrus would need a leader, would need to have one man to follow —and now he carried two empty shells in his pocket, to make him remember. Once, Simbele knew that he would have done the same himself; but now he had chosen something different and he would make himself forget that other man's face and voice.

But there would be changes, he knew; he sat back in his chair and as coldly as he could thought them out. There would be at least two very important changes; first, they have decided that it does not matter if they harm their own people—oh, it is true that they killed black policemen before, but to be a policeman at all meant that you were turning your back on the people. But the killing of the four convicts showed that they had decided that if necessary their own people should suffer as much as the white people. For those convicts, as Simbele knew, were probably people serving short sentences, for some petty offence, who were looking forward to release and perhaps a return to their families; or perhaps they had been afraid. But neither of those reasons would be sufficient to kill them.

Second, Simbele knew that the decision to stay on in the mountains and not to seek at least temporary asylum over the border meant that they were turning this into a suicide mission; or perhaps they believed that the local black people were ready to rise up in a full-scale rebellion. Simbele knew that if it were the latter it was not convincing—the people were oppressed, all right, and they knew that they were oppressed. But they were not ready to fight the merciless civil war that an uprising proper would entail; and who could say that they were not right? They saw enough of the police and soldiers to realize what the odds were—and most ordinary people would not see the point of a useless sacrifice, no matter how oppressed they were. Could the new leader suppose that the time for such an uprising was now? Surely he could not be so foolish, so out of touch with the real feelings of people in the region? So perhaps what he planned was terrorism of the suicidal kind, the daylight attacks on white people, the attacks on the focal points of the towns, the police-station, the ambushing of cars on the road—in short, all the methods of terrorism proper. Would that have any real effect, Simbele wondered; would it create the kind of conditions that might lead to a revolution? He did not know, but he doubted it. Yet he knew at the same time that it made no difference to him; even if he disagreed with the new methods that the new leader might persuade his men to, he had chosen and so he belonged to everything that they did; and the difference in methods was one of degree, not kind, so he would stay with them, he would do what he was asked to, he would serve this cause that he no longer was sure of, this cause, which he had once decided was necessary, which he could no longer justify, even to himself, or especially to himself—for he did not have to justify it to anyone else—but which he was a part of, by his own original choice.

He had admired the old leader, had liked what little he knew of him, had respected him, but he was prepared to follow the new leader. If he had been a complete member of the group, if he had been sweating through the mountains now, watching every bush and every cloud, then he might have the right to object; perhaps even if he was like his pupil Petrus he might have the right, because Petrus had been with them and had seen terrible things with them. But Simbele knew that he himself was on the outside, and so he had no rights to control what they did—it was not an argument that he would very much have liked to defend on reasonable grounds, but he felt the force of it in himself. Always he had the right to stay with them up there in the mountains, not to return to his other life; but always he returned.

Simbele, standing next to his desk in the classroom, looked down the neat rows of chairs and tables, desks for the senior pupils, benches for the rest; there was something about an empty classroom that suited his mood these days—often he would sit for hours after he had dismissed the children; sometimes he would pretend to work, but more often he would just stare into the room. Then he would grow impatient with himself, would stand up, and would walk towards the door; but usually he would discover that he had forgotten to do something, and an hour later he would still be there, either working at his desk or wandering around the room, looking at what his pupils had done that day. In some other country, he thought, he would have enjoyed being a teacher; sometimes he enjoyed it even here; but there was always the sense that you were educating people to take their fixed place, and it was not their place. There would be time for teaching later, even though he was not likely to be around to do it himself. There would be others, however; that boy Petrus, he would make a good teacher one day—not a very clever one perhaps, but a good one, sincere, strong, believing in other people, believing in what he did, believing that what he taught his pupils made a difference to them in the world. There would be a time for that later; what you had to do now was to wait; and what you were waiting for would not take long, not long before it came.

* * *

Mrs. Allen too was waiting. She was not absolutely certain what she was waiting for, since that was in part of her mind that she dared not examine, but she was sure that she was waiting for something; she was not impatient; she was entirely content to wait—for she was sure that whatever she was waiting for would not be long in coming. It was not simply that somewhere in her mind she felt that something was coming; it seemed to her that throughout the settlement there was the same mood of waiting, patient waiting, sullen waiting, just as men besieged but expecting relief must watch the horizon for the movement of dust that means it is coming, just as a farmer in a drought watches the massed clouds, not daring to hope for a storm, but waiting all the same, knowing that eventually it must come. It was not really hope that she felt, any more than the mood in the settlement was one of hope—but then, neither was it despair, for the certainty that something was coming made despair seem too passive an emotion for her; for, though she was resigned to waiting, it was not in a spirit of resignation that she waited.

In the meantime, she did her work as well as she knew how, and as hard as she could. She had to spend more time in the hospital than before, partly because there was no Dr. Redman, partly because Nurse Peters had left and her replacement, though an amiable soul, was very slow and needed careful teaching before she understood her duties. Mrs. Allen took on a great deal of the more ordinary nursing work herself, helping Sister Mbele deal with outpatients, helping decide when the doctor should be summoned to deal with the worst cases, helping with the dispensing, even helping with the cleaning. She re-started the crèche which had been allowed to lapse during her absence. She found the school children whom she had paid to water the dust every day, criticized them for having fallen down on their job so quickly, and then doubled their wages on condition that they did the job properly again. She planted more succulents and aloes in the small rockery that she had had built outside her cottage.

She made one nearly disastrous mistake. Without consulting anyone, she decided that it really was time that old Joseph was pensioned off. She could see that he was getting slower and slower every day; he dug the graves so painfully slowly that she was worried that one day one of the old people of the settlement might die and there would be no grave ready; and you couldn't leave anybody long before you buried him, even in the small mortuary next to the hospital. Yes, she was sure that old Joseph had to retire, had to be retired, if necessary. She tried to explain to him herself, though she expected that he would not understand; standing among the graves, she told him, in very simple words, repeating each sentence carefully, that, as from the next Monday, he need not continue his work; she had arranged, she said, for a younger man to do the job from now on. The old man laughed throughout her speech and went on digging, pitifully, she thought, scratching at the hard ground of the hillside.

But she was determined; and on the Monday morning she and the new gravedigger—a middle-aged man who had returned permanently from the phosphate mines a few months before—went up to the cemetery to relieve old Joseph. But even when the man spoke to him, on Mrs. Allen's instructions, in Tswana, he still didn't seem to understand, still went on with his feeble digging; so Mrs. Allen sent the new man to get another spade from the Superintendent's houseboy. She waited, watching old Joseph still scratching away at the loose stones and the dry earth, until the man came back with the spade, and then showed him where to dig, before herself going back down to the settlement to ask Simbele if he would mind leaving his class for a few moments to come to explain to old Joseph that he was to be pensioned off. But before she reached the school, the man came running after her, blood pouring from a jagged cut in the crown of his head. While she took him to the surgery and herself cleaned the wound and bandaged his head, he explained that he had started digging, as she had told him to; old Joseph, seeing this interloper, must have abandoned his own digging to stalk quietly up behind the new man, and, before he could escape, struck him savagely over the head with his spade, "like a mad thing", the man said, "like a strong man gone mad."

When Mrs. Allen tried to persuade him to go back with her to the cemetery to remonstrate with old Joseph, he refused point-blank; he wanted nothing more to do with the job under any circumstances. Furious at his cowardice, Mrs. Allen tried to force him to come with her; but sullenly he refused, and when she tried, later, to find someone else to take old Joseph's place, she found that the story of the attack had spread around the settlement and that there was not a single man prepared to do it.

So she went to Simbele for advice; he told her, as gently as he could, that he felt that she had been mistaken in trying to pension old Joseph off. "He's been here so long, you see," he explained, "that if you stopped him working, he'd probably die tomorrow." Mrs. Allen had to accept what he said, although secretly she wished that she could find another man at least to help old Joseph.

But, if her attempt to replace old Joseph was nearly a disastrous mistake, she knew that her going to Simbele for advice had been very sensible. It seemed to her that his entire attitude to her had changed and that he was at last prepared to be friendly to her. So she asked him for advice again, this time in choosing a successor to Nurse Peters, who had been the one the Bishop had mentioned as having gone off without warning; at first Simbele had refused, but later, although she did not press him, he came to the hospital one afternoon to tell her that he had talked to Sister Mbele and that they both felt that Mrs. Bereng would be the best choice. Mrs. Allen accepted the advice gladly, and, a day or two later, risked going to visit the school while classes were in progress. This time, the children had been prepared to return to their work when Simbele told them to, and she was able to wander round the classroom, while the children went on working, and was even able to talk to one or two of the less shy pupils. After that, Mrs. Allen considered inviting Simbele to tea; but after much thought she decided that she should wait. There would be time for that later, she thought.

So, generally, she returned as closely as was possible to her routine before ever it had been upset. She still hardly ever saw the Superintendent, not even at the evening meal now, for he seemed to be living almost permanently in a hotel in Verderdorp, and drove out to the settlement every morning and back again every evening. Not that he need worry to come, thought Mrs. Allen—he does almost nothing while he is here, except to hold a weekly meeting with the so-called committee at which nothing is decided. His houseboy still cleaned his house meticulously every day, and Mrs. Allen imagined that the Superintendent must eventually intend to come back there, for one day she saw the houseman painting it again, as he had been doing when she first arrived. That seemed to her a bit much to tolerate, that paint should be wasted on a house that was hardly ever lived in; so she made a point, next time she saw the Superintendent, of going across to him (and she suspected that he saw her coming, pretending not to notice her, and walked faster) and of asking him if he could not allow his houseboy to come to repaint the exterior of the hospital, since the paint was flaking away and the original white was now a khaki-grey, almost the colour of the dust itself.

"Oh no, he couldn't do that," the Superintendent answered. "He has a great deal to do in my house."

"But you are never there," Mrs. Allen said, laughingly.

Very formally he answered her, "If you have any complaints about my work, you must please make them direct to the Minister of Bantu Administration."

"Oh, I have no complaints," Mrs. Allen said—really, this man is absurd, she thought; an incompetent coward.

"Very well, Mrs. Allen," the Superintendent replied. Then he looked round to see that no one could possibly hear, although they were in fact standing right in the middle of the dust-bowl, and leaned confidentially forward to say, "You see, Mrs. Allen, the police have told me that it is not safe to stay here while there are those terrorists around."

"Really, Superintendent?" she replied; but the irony seemed lost on him, for he nodded and said, "Yes, until the police catch these men, it would not be safe for me to stay here."

And what about me, thought Mrs. Allen; don't I exist to you? Am I so insubstantial that terrorists' bullets would pass through me, or have I such protection of the gods that their bullets would turn to water? Yet she could not feel anger towards him, he was so pitifully afraid; nor was there any point in complaining about his uselessness—she had been tempted to before, but though now he was doing even less for the settlement than he had done before, there was not so much reason to complain and nothing that a complaint would achieve—indeed, she felt almost glad that he was so useless, for it meant that there would be no interference in her own effort.

In some strange way, perhaps because she had not been herself when it happened, it felt almost as if Dr. Redman had not died at all, as if he had simply gone away. Sister Mbele had given her all the details that she had been too ill to comprehend —how they had put Dr. Redman's body in the mortuary, how Nurse Peters had refused to allow the other nurses in but had washed his body herself, how the police surgeon had come in and had done a post-mortem examination to make sure of the cause of death, how Redman's parents had flown to Johannesburg and had taken a car out, the old man crying, the mother silent and dry-eyed, how they had sent to Verderdorp for a funeral car and had driven off behind it on the long journey back to Cape Town. Yet the details had not appalled Mrs. Allen, as she would have expected them to, for she seemed, even to herself, unable to connect the Dr. Redman she had known with the man who had died out there in the fields, sweating his way into the short coma that imperceptibly became death. Yet she did not feel that he was still alive in the way that Terry was still alive to her; for there was nothing about Dr. Redman that made her feel that automatically he must have triumphed over death, particularly because he had killed himself, had not been prepared to face the consequences of his own actions—or perhaps because he had embraced death so willingly, rather as if he were going as a guest to its house. Mrs. Allen could not help believing that if you were not afraid of death, it meant that you had some sort of conception of life after death—she was not at all an intellectual woman, she had no reasonable grounds for her belief but she understood in some other way than intellectually; she felt that death was not the ending. Terry went on in some way, she was not sure how, but he went on. Dr. Redman perhaps went on in some similar way, a way that she could neither understand nor feel. It was all very muddled, what was inside her, but something was there just as much as something was coming, just as much as she was waiting for something to come.

XIII

What Simbele expected to happen did happen—and soon. First, one of the terrorists went to the house of the local Commissioner of Police dressed like a man out of work, asked for work, was told by the black maid that there was none to be had, drew a revolver and shot her dead. He went into the house and shot the Commissioner's wife and her four-year-old son. A neighbour, hearing the shots, phoned the police. They arrived to find that the terrorist was still there, for he shot one of the policemen who came running up the path to see what had happened. The others radioed for reinforcements and, when they came, drew the attention of the man away with a decoy and shot him with a rifle from the roof of a neighbouring building.

Then two terrorists went one night to the house of one of the senior black policemen in Verderdorp, called him out, walked him into the fields just outside the township where he lived, and shot him. They were not caught.

Then a single terrorist, armed only with a grenade, went to Verderdorp one Saturday night, went to the white cinema, forced his way past the doorkeeper and the manager, and threw the grenade inside. Four people were killed and eleven injured, six of them seriously. Before the police arrived, some of the uninjured people caught the terrorist, who made little attempt to escape, and beat him to death.

The police had already been empowered to arrest anyone on the remotest suspicion of knowledge of terrorism; no charges were needed, no evidence, and there was no legal way of preventing such detention. Partly to allay the fears of the white population—for there was a rumour that the terrorists planned to poison the Verderdorp reservoir—the police used these powers now to arrest a group of thirty Africans—the police headquarters in Pretoria issued a press statement that the people had been arrested on suspicion of assisting the terrorists, but they were in fact hostages, taken at random from farms and townships in the region, and held in the police cells in Verderdorp. The group included eight women and six children.

From the settlement the police took five hostages, either because they still suspected that Dr. Redman's involvement with the terrorists meant that there was some deeper connection between the terrorists and the settlement, or because they simply distrusted the settlement as the kind of place that fomented revolution. They came early one morning, just after dawn, called together all the Africans there, told them that they were taking five of them away to make sure that the terrorists knew who would really suffer as a result of their actions, and then sent two black policemen into the crowd to select the five hostages, two men, two women, and an eight-year-old boy, one of Simbele's pupils. To Mrs. Allen who was called from her quarters by one of the old men on the committee, the police said that her protests were useless; they had been ordered to take five people from the settlement and they were taking five people, whatever she said. When she said that she would ask the Superintendent as soon as he arrived to phone the Minister of Bantu Administration to protest, the police laughed at her and explained that they had got permission from the Superintendent at his hotel the night before to come to the settlement to make the arrests. Mrs. Allen watched the police van with its load of hostages leaving, then turned on the waiting crowd to scream at them, "And you will just let them do it to you! Why don't you do something, one of you, why doesn't one of you make some effort to prevent this? For God's sake, if any of you know of the terrorists, tell the police, tell me, so that we can get our people back." The crowd stared at her silently and then, in small groups, began to turn away to walk to their huts on the edge of the circle of the dust-bowl. Seeing Simbele too walking away through the crowd, Mrs. Allen ran after him, clutched at his arm, and said to him, "Mr. Simbele, surely there is something we can do? There must be something we can do. We can't just let these people be taken away for no reason—everybody knows that they haven't done anything."

Simbele shrugged. "What can we do?" he asked.

"Can't we get them lawyers or something?"

"Mrs. Allen," he said as gently as he could. "There may be laws for you—there is only one law for us; the police. What the police want is our law."

"But that's wrong, it's wrong," she cried at him. He only smiled a strange little half-smile at her and walked away, slowly through the dust.

* * *

That night Simbele left the settlement and went to join the terrorists. He didn't know where they were, but he was sure that Petrus would be able to guide him.

* * *

Two days later, the terrorists, with Simbele and Petrus among them, attacked the police station at Verderdorp. The press statement issued by police headquarters in Pretoria after the attack gave out that six of the hostages had been killed by the terrorists during the attack; in fact, they had been killed by a young policeman who, the moment the attack started, went round behind the police station and sprinted to the cells, where he lined the six men in the first cell up against the wall and walked down the row, shooting each one in the back of the head. He had forgotten to take more ammunition with him and so he killed no more, for he was shot through both legs on his return journey to reload his revolver and lay in the courtyard, moaning for help, until the terrorists were beaten off.

For an hour or so it seemed, however, that the terrorists would succeed. The police station was not in a very defensible position, certainly, for it was on a street corner, its front facing the main road just before it forked, one road leading on to Grysberg, one road veering off towards the south and Johannesburg. Across the road were a number of shops, mainly general dealers whose customers were the local black people—the whites shopped farther up the main road—across the side road on the west was a small newsagent's shop and a private house, to the east was a wrecker's yard full of derelict cars and, next to that, a garage. To the south was the police playing field. The police station itself was a red-brick double storey building, a simple box shape, and immediately behind it was the courtyard, open on both sides. Then there were the cells, in a single-storey building of the same red brick, with a small enclosed courtyard to the east of it. Behind the cells was a small strip of garden, kept meticulously by one of the regular prisoners, and then a low white building that served both as accommodation for off-duty policemen and for bachelors' quarters. Behind the barracks was the playing field.

The new leader had told them in the mountains before they left on the long walk to Verderdorp that the plan was to launch a minor frontal attack on the actual police station, to keep the police confined to the building both by that and by firing from the shelter of the wrecker's yard and from the newsagent's shop, across the open courtyard immediately behind the police station, while the main body of men moved up across the playing field to take the barracks and so to get to the cells to release the hostages. It was, as far as Simbele could tell, a perfectly well-conceived attack and, with a little more luck, it would have succeeded, for the frontal attack succeeded in drawing the attention of the police entirely to the front of the building, and would have brought all the men resting or sleeping in the barracks—for the attack was timed for just after dawn, so that the terrorists could come into town with the usual black workers going in from the township to the houses and factories of their employers—except for the fact that the cross-fire from the newsagent's shop and the wrecker's yard was so fierce that it not only prevented the police leaving the building where they were on duty but also drove the off-duty policemen to retreat again to the barracks, where they were able to put up stiff resistance to the main body of terrorists attacking from the south across the playing field. Within minutes the group attacking from the south was pinned down by the revolver and rifle fire of the police in the barracks; they were relatively safe, however, since they had the trees and the bank of the playing field to take cover behind. With that group tied down, with the group which had carried out the diversionary frontal attack almost wiped out except for four men, two of them wounded, and so unable to do any more than to ensure that the police did not try to break out of the front, and with only two small groups of terrorists on the east and the west, the attack was a failure; for, although the police were trapped, the terrorists knew that, unless they managed to take at least the barracks immediately, they would not have long before the police managed to call up reinforcements.

Simbele and Petrus were two of the four men sent to flank the attack from the wrecker's yard on the east. They had walked in to Verderdorp from the township, the two of them together in the half-light and small wind of very early dawn, carrying their rifles wrapped in sacks and newspapers, trying to pretend that what they carried were sticks or shovels or pick-axes; the workmen cycling and walking along the same dusty road had looked at them strangely, but asked no questions. When they reached the wrecker's yard from which they had been told to watch over the back of the main police station, they stopped for a moment and then turned quickly to duck through the gate and into the yard.

"Hey," the black garage attendant called as they did so. "Hey, you can't go in there." But they went on, as quickly as they could, while he rushed in through the gate after them, calling on them to stop. Petrus and Simbele waited until they were safely in among the wrecked cars and trucks before they did stop to allow the man to catch them up.

"Look," said the man. "You can't come in here. Nobody is allowed to."

"Go away," said Petrus fiercely. "Go away before you get hurt." He lifted his rifle above his head as if it were a club.

"If they find you here," the attendant said, "I shall be sacked."

"Go away," said Petrus, still with the covered rifle raised. "Go away," and he moved a threatening step closer. Simbele, behind him, fumbled with the sacking and newspaper that disguised his rifle, got it off, and raised the rifle to his shoulder, pointing it at the attendant. For a moment the man didn't seem to see it and, when he did, he said nothing, simply turned and ran, looking back over his shoulder every few yards, as he ducked in and out of the motor cars.

"All right," said Simbele to Petrus. "All right; now wait. It won't be long now."

"Won't he tell the police?" Petrus said, gesturing towards where the attendant had disappeared.

"Perhaps," said Simbele, and shrugged. "It's too late to worry now, Petrus." He smiled at the boy, then said, "You haven't changed your mind about coming?"

Petrus shook his head; he knew that Simbele was not suggesting that he might be afraid, for Simbele had argued with him for hours on end, first, to persuade him to go back to the settlement and his mother and, later, simply to dissuade him from joining the attack. There had been little use in it; Simbele knew that in these things the boy was almost, as it were, older than he himself was—and he had been so on fire with the idea of action that he had not listened to a word that Simbele had said, had simply looked steadily back into his face, as if he had a certainty that went beyond argument, beyond words, beyond the desire for action even, a certainty as a man fighting a blood-feud might have.

"Well, then," said Simbele, now unconsciously speaking in the tones of a schoolmaster, "Perhaps we should find good positions for ourselves."

Petrus chose a big black Chevrolet without wheels or bonnet or engine, and installed himself in the front seat where he had a clear view of the back of the main police station and the courtyard in front of the windowless line of cells. Simbele sheltered behind a rusty old five-ton truck; he didn't trust himself to shoot straight for, although they had told him how to fire the rifle, he had not actually been able to fire it at all, for fear that the noise might reveal their last hiding place in the mountains. Within a minute or two, two other men came up from the rear of the wrecker's yard and took up similar positions—one of them had an automatic rifle, not like those which Simbele and Petrus had, but a larger, shinier affair, and the other carried a submachine gun; both waved to Simbele and Petrus and the one with the machine gun pretended to shoot at Petrus through the window of his car; Simbele could see him smiling. Then they took up similar positions.

* * *

Five minutes later, the frontal attack started when a hand grenade was hurled through a window into the charge office. As they had been instructed to do, the four men in the wrecker's yard held their fire until they saw a policeman come running, crouched over like a baboon, out of the door of the police station and across the yard, for they saw him fall and saw him writhing on the concrete courtyard. But now they were under fire themselves, from the upper windows of the east side of the police station; Simbele could hear the clunk clunk clunk of bullets hitting the metalwork of the derelict cars, the occasional whine of a ricochet, and then the rattle as the man on his left fired his sub-machine gun, driving whoever was firing at them back. He could see Petrus, crouched in the front of the Chevrolet, firing carefully; what was he shooting at, Simbele wondered. He could not see anyone or anything to fire at and there seemed little point in firing at the windows. He put his rifle carefully down, fumbled in his pocket, took out the cigarette that he had been saving for this moment, and lit it. The sun was up now; he knew that if he turned round he would see it, huge and flaming behind him—but he did not turn. Suddenly he felt completely at peace, felt almost happy; he put his cigarette in the corner of his mouth, picked up his rifle again, and, with the smoke of the cigarette making his eyes water, fired one careful shot at one of the windows of the police station; he saw the glass shatter, and he laughed—yes, he was happy. As the police began to fire again, raking across the wrecker's yard, trying to pick out their attackers, Simbele went on firing at each window in turn, trying deliberately to smash each one, not really caring that there were men behind, just aiming to break each one of those shiny panes.

Suddenly he realized that the man with the sub-machine gun had stopped firing. He ducked down and looked along the lane between the cars; the man was sitting in the dust, crouched over, his hands clutched across his chest, like a man praying— the gun was lying a yard or two in front of him. Simbele put his own rifle down carefully and, bent double, ran across the open space between his shelter and the man: kneeling down next to him, he knew that the police had seen him running in the open, and he knew that the burst of firing he heard as he ran had been aimed at him; and the clunk clunk clunk of bullets on the car behind which he crouched were meant as a very private song for him. The man, he could see, was badly wounded, although he made no sound; there was blood and something else that Simbele did not dare look at under his crossed hands; and there was blood coming out of his mouth. The man looked at Simbele and seemed to smile, then nodded his head. Simbele, still kneeling, turned round and picked up the sub-machine gun; as he did so he heard the man fall sideways and when he looked at him again he knew that he was dead.

With the sub-machine gun in his left hand, Simbele ran back to his old position, hearing again the clunk clunk clunk of the bullets that the police fired especially for him; he didn't know how to use the gun and he didn't have any more ammunition for it, but he had better try to finish up whatever ammunition was still in it. He picked it up, cradled it against his shoulder, aimed it roughly at the window from which at least one of the policemen was firing at them, and pulled the trigger—he heard that it was working though he did not know if he was hitting anything. He knew that he could probably use the rifle more effectively; but it seemed right to use this gun instead.

Someone was calling him. He looked over to Petrus to see that he had left the front of the Chevrolet and was crouching behind the car. The boy was signalling, pointing down the lane between the cars, pointing over behind Simbele. He looked round; there was someone coming up there, crawling and rushing from cover to cover in short bursts of speed. Simbele called out to Petrus, "Wait until I begin firing, then come here." He stood up, with the gun against his shoulder, and began to sweep the side of the police station, window to window to window, driving the police back into shelter, while Petrus came over the open ground to join him. Simbele went on firing until the gun was suddenly silent in his hands. Petrus and the man who had been approaching were both with him now, crouching in the dust behind the truck.

"Thank you for the cover," the man said. Simbele looked at him; he was the man with the scar, the new leader. Quickly he looked at Petrus; the boy's face was set firm, mouth tight, eyes steady.

"Where are the other two?" the leader asked.

Simbele pointed at the dead man in the dust. "And the other?" the leader asked.

"I don't know," said Petrus, looking at Simbele rather than at the man. "He stopped shooting very early on."

"All right," said the leader. "Well, listen. We are stuck at the back there—we can't get into the barracks. So what we are going to do is this: in ten minutes or so we are going to try to get up that side road, you know, the other side there, and into the police station itself through the back." He gestured to explain, and then quickly sketched the route in the dust. "When you see our men come round there," and he pointed to the corner of the cells, "to cross that courtyard, you must fire above them, at the top windows. Do you understand?"

Simbele and Petrus nodded. "Good," said the man. "Now, I have to get round to the front there. Will you cover me again? I have to get to the front and then round to the newsagent's shop." He smiled at them and said, "You are doing very well, schoolteacher and pupil." Simbele noticed that Petrus did not smile back.

"I'm ready," said the man, getting up into a crouching position. Simbele grabbed his rifle and he and Petrus stood up to begin firing again. As the man sprinted across the open space, Simbele saw Petrus, standing next to him, turn slightly and fire twice, carefully, at the bent back of the leader. For a moment or two, Simbele thought that Petrus had missed, for the man seemed to keep running for several yards, but then, as if he had tripped, he fell forwards into the dust. Before Simbele could stop him, Petrus stood up and, with his rifle swinging from his left hand, walked out, quite casually, into the open space towards the fallen body. He walked to the body and Simbele saw the boy fumble in his pocket, produce something from it, look at it cupped in his hand for a moment, and drop whatever it was in the dust next to the body; and Simbele knew then that what the boy had dropped there in the dust were the two empty and shining cartridge cases that he had kept ever since the killing of the old leader, had kept for this moment when they could be returned, with vengeance for four dead convicts and one dead leader. As Simbele watched, Petrus turned, and began to walk back, still as slowly as if he had been walking over the fields, and he was half way back before the first bullet hit him, spinning him round. Then, as he seemed to regain his balance, another bullet hit him directly in the face, knocking him yards backwards and into the dust.

* * *

Ten minutes later, the attack that they had been told about started. Simbele heard the sudden increase of fighting, and a moment or two later saw the first of their men come round the corner of the cells and towards the back door of the police station. Frantically he fired at the upper windows for he could see men there; but within a moment or two it was obvious that the attack would fail for as each man came into the courtyard he seemed to stumble and fall; then there were no men coming round the corner of the building and there were only the heaped bodies in the courtyard.

Simbele put down his rifle against the side of the truck. Carefully, steadily, he emptied his pockets of ammunition and untied the handkerchief which he had round his neck to catch the sweat. Then, without looking at the bodies in the dust, he began to crawl away from his truck towards the side of the yard. Nobody seemed to be firing at him any more and he reached the wooden railings quite easily; he crawled a little way along until he found a small gap and slithered through. With the wooden fence between him and the police station he could walk upright. He went in through the back of the garage and found his way through to the front. It was completely deserted. The attendant was lying on the concrete near one of the petrol pumps, his arms and legs sprawled; there was blood on his clothes and on the concrete. Simbele stopped to look at him and then walked on up the main road that led into the white shopping area. There was no one else on the streets at all and even the firing behind him seemed to have stopped.

* * *

Of the policemen, eight were killed and five injured. Of the terrorists, twenty-seven were killed; the police shot all the wounded as they found them. Four by-standers were killed, including the garage attendant. Fifteen terrorists were captured; of these, twelve were executed within an hour of their capture, in the courtyard behind the police station. Two of them the police kept for a show trial; they kept Simbele, too, who had been taken at a road block two hundred yards down the main road by three policemen who had been out on a routine patrol when the attack started and who, very sensibly, had decided that the best thing they could do was to set up a road block to prevent anyone getting to the attack or away from it. He had been taken back to the police station and lined up with the rest of the men against the wall of the courtyard, while the police chose the two men to keep for the trial; and he would have been shot with the rest of them, if one of the policemen had not recognized him as the teacher from the settlement. He was pulled out of the line, his hands were tied together in front of him with a long piece of rope, and he was made to watch the execution of the twelve men. Then a machine gun was mounted in the back of one open land-rover truck, two white policemen got into the front, and Simbele was made to climb into the back of another truck with two black policemen, one of whom looped the rope that tied Simbele's hands together round his neck and who amused himself on the dusty drive to the settlement by half-throttling him at regular intervals.

XIV

Listening to the nine o'clock news that morning, Mrs. Allen heard that there had been an attack by the terrorists on the Verderdorp police station—troops were being flown in, said the report, to make sure that there was no chance of large-scale danger to the population, although the police had the situation well in hand. Before details of the attack were given, a joint statement by the Ministers of National Security and of Bantu Administration was read out, which, in one sense, tried to play the incident down, for fear of creating panic and, in another sense, tried to play it up, for the sake of justifying the earlier declaration of a state of emergency in the region. Then details were given, the number of terrorists killed—the twelve men executed were simply added to the total, without a mention of execution—but details of police deaths and injuries were not given. At the end of the report, the announcer said that six of the thirty prisoners who were being held in the cells during the attack had been killed—the unstated assumption was that the terrorists had killed them.

Carefully, Mrs. Allen turned off the radio—she guessed immediately that the "six of the thirty prisoners who were being held in the cells" were hostages. Had any of them been from the settlement, she wondered; and had the terrorists really killed them? It didn't seem very likely, she knew; but she also knew that it didn't matter who had killed them—without a doubt they had been innocent, and they were dead. She walked from the kitchen to her bedroom, took a hand-written letter from the table she used as a desk, walked back to the kitchen, and burnt the letter. There was no point in sending it now, for it was a letter to the Minister of Bantu Administration protesting against the inhumanity of the police's taking innocent hostages, women and children at that. She had spent the last two evenings composing the letter, had been so involved in it that she had hardly noticed that Simbele and Mrs. Mbele's son were missing—and, anyway, she hadn't worried, not like Sister Mbele had worried, for she trusted Simbele implicitly—and because at the last minute she had not been sure of the wording, she had left the letter on her desk, to read that morning again. It hadn't been an easy letter to write, for she wanted on the one hand to make her protest powerful and on the other she knew that, if she made it too powerful, it would have the effect not of gaining the Minister's sympathy but of alienating him. She had known anyway that it was likely to be a futile gesture, though she also knew that its probable futility was no excuse for not doing it—had not Terry always said that was a great evil, to be so convinced that your efforts would fail that you did not make the effort at all? Her effort had not had the chance to fail; it had just been too late.

She sat down again at the kitchen table; it is a quarter past nine, she noticed—she should have been at the hospital, but oh how weary she was. There doesn't seem to be any end to this, she thought; you crossed from circle to circle, and there was still another circle, and then still another circle. Yet how horribly wrong those men were, she said to herself, to believe that you could end hatred by creating more hatred, end disease by killing the diseased; whoever thought that you could feed the hungry on blood, clothe the naked by lining them against a wall, and comfort the sick by locking them away? Oh, how wrong they were; and remembering the dead terrorists whose eyes she had closed, and her dreams of the dead and mutilated policemen, she pitied them—oh, how wrong they were, she murmured again, and the voices took up the words, and first repeated them, and then began to change them, and to shout different words, and to curse and to scream, until Mrs. Allen was forced to hurry herself across the dust-bowl to the hospital, to her work, not noticing the small groups of people gathering quietly among the huts on the far side of the settlement.

Ten minutes later, she was in the dispensary, carefully checking the supplies of drugs, down on her hands and knees next to the cupboard, checking names, counting bottles, dusting them, replacing them, marking the meticulous inventory, when suddenly the door of the room was flung open and Sister Mbele burst in. Mrs. Allen looked up in surprise—"You know that I don't like your coming in here without . . ." she began to say, but Sister Mbele, catching her breath, and crying, and interrupting, cried out, "They've caught Simbele."

"Who has 'caught' Simbele?"

"The police, the police—they've caught Simbele," she was crying hysterically.

"How do you know?" Mrs. Allen asked—but the woman was so out of control, half-weeping, half-laughing, that there was no sense to be got from her. "Pull yourself together, Sister," Mrs. Allen said, and when this had no effect, she stood up and slapped her hard across the cheek: it was a long time since she had used such a remedy for hysteria, but it seemed only to make the woman more idiotic. So Mrs. Allen shook her by the shoulders until she regained her senses and was able to speak; as she did so she shouted, "How do you know? Where is he? Where are the police?" at the shaking, helpless woman, who made no answer but simply gestured at the window.

"What do you mean? Is he here? Is that it? Is he here? Have they brought him here? Why have they brought him? Has he done something wrong?" Mrs. Allen screamed at the woman question after question, and still got no reply, only the helpless, deep-throated, keening wail. Remembering then, Mrs. Allen shouted, "And where's Petrus? Do you know where Petrus is now?" But still there was only the helpless crying, so abandoning her attempt to make the woman speak sense, Mrs. Allen ran to the door. The sister still stood there, weeping hysterically; Mrs. Allen ran back, grabbed her arm, and tugged her forward. "Come on, you great blubbering fool. What can you do here?" she said, but the woman refused to move, simply stood still there in the middle of the kitchen, wailing to herself in some private hell in which there was nothing that anybody could do.

Cursing under her breath, Mrs. Allen rushed to the door, threw it open, ran down the corridor, slipping on the polished floor at the corner, down the passage again and then through the open glass door, and then through the mesh door, and stopping short as she looked out into the dust-bowl.

Standing there in the middle of the bowl were all the people of the settlement, gathered into a tight circle above which the dust rose and eddied like a cloud. Mrs. Allen was at first not able to see just what it was that they were gathered to see, but then she saw, in the centre of the crowd, and slightly above the heads of the people, a police land-rover—and then another police land-rover. As she ran stumbling across the dust-bowl, she saw that on the central land-rover three people were standing, one white and two black; closer, she could see that two were policemen and one was not; closer, the man in between the policemen was Simbele, very tall, very thin. She ran across the dust-bowl, the dust flying up, choking her, blinding her, into the crowd, pushing roughly through, cursing, shoving, bullying her way through, until the people realized who she was and parted for her.

When she got to the front of the crowd, five yards away from the land-rover, she realized that the police were speaking to the crowd—or rather, that the white policeman was speaking in Afrikaans, the black man was translating into Tswana; she could understand only a few words of what the white man said, nothing of what the black man translated. "What's he saying?"

she asked the man next to her urgently, "What's he saying? I can't understand." But the man shrugged, as if to say, I hear, but do not listen. She looked frantically around for someone she recognized, but everyone seemed a stranger. She looked up at Simbele, only five or six yards away from her, but he did not look at her; he stood, very tall although his head was bowed, his hands clasped in front of him, between the policemen, the white man away from him, the black man near; and, looking at him, she realized suddenly that his hands were tied, that there was a rope round his neck, a rope that occasionally the black policeman would raise in the air to gesture in emphasis of something that he said. The white policeman made no gestures as he spoke.

"What's he saying?" she asked her neighbours again, frantically. Some of them looked at her but nobody replied—indeed, it seemed to her that they looked at her as if she were not there. She stepped forward out of the crowd, to go up to the policeman; as she did so the white policeman behind the machine-gun on the other land-rover swung it round to point at her and a black policeman, standing casually between the land-rover and the crowd, stepped forward and roughly pushed her back into the crowd.

"Take your hands off me, you filthy beast," she cried out, without thinking. He smiled and pushed her again, back into the crowd. She had to do something, she knew that she had to do something. "Can't you do something?" she said to the people around her; and they stared at her as if she spoke a language they did not understand. So she turned and ran back through the crowd, pushing her way angrily through, out into the open and then across the dust-bowl to the Superintendent's office. He was sitting at his desk, which was bare except for his revolver, and he started to his feet, grabbing at the gun, as she burst in. When he saw who it was he sighed with relief and sat down again.

"Do you know what's going on out there?" Mrs. Allen, furious, asked him.

"Yes," he said. "Who would have believed that Simbele could do a thing like that? It only goes to show—you cannot trust any one of them, especially the educated ones."

"For God's sake," she shouted now. "Are you going to sit there and let these swine do what they want to one of your own people?"

"Simbele may be your people," he said with heavy sarcasm, "He's not mine."

"He works for you, doesn't he?"

"He used to."

"And you will let the police do what they want now? My God, have you no loyalty at all?"

"Loyalty to what, Mrs. Allen? Do you know what that man is—he is a murderer, and the blood is not dry on his hands. The police can do what they want to him; the worst they can do will not be bad enough for him."

"Simbele's not a murderer—he couldn't possibly be one."

"He is, Mrs. Allen, he is . . .", but she would not allow him to finish.

"You are a cowardly and incompetent fool, Mr. Schwartz," she said carefully, and then repeated it so that he would get the meaning of each word perfectly clear. Before he could reply, she was out of the office, running again, running towards the crowd, running frantically still. Once again she had to fight her way through the crowd, pushing and shoving and barging and using her elbows to make a path for herself through the shoulder to shoulder people. They were still all strangers; it seemed to her that she had never seen one of them before. They were still absolutely quiet; only the dust rising from the involuntary movements of their feet showed that they were alive. Mrs. Allen pushed straight through the crowd and out into the small open space in the middle; once again the white policeman behind the machine-gun swung it round to point it at her, and once again the black policeman stepped forward and started to push her back into the crowd. This time she slapped him, as hard as she could across the face. He grabbed her wrist and, bending it back, started to force her to her knees. The crowd behind her sighed, as a forest sighs before a storm. The machine-gun swung restlessly across the crowd, the policeman each side of Simbele stopped speaking, and one bent down and picked up a tommy gun at his feet and cradled it casually to his waist. Another white policeman jumped down from the cab of the land-rover truck, came up to where the black policeman was smilingly watching Mrs. Allen slowly being forced down into a kneeling position as he pressed her wrist back, and hit the policeman as hard as he could in the face. Again the crowd sighed. The black policeman moved a yard or two back, his hands held to his head, and Mrs. Allen slowly stood up again.

The white policeman who had rescued her was Sergeant Van der Post; she recognized him from the time of her breakdown as the man who had helped question her, the man who had been least unpleasant to her.

"What's happening?" she asked him.

"We caught that man Johannes," and he gestured with his head at Simbele.

"You mean Simbele."

"Yes, that's his name."

"What's he done?"

"He was one of the terrorists who attacked the police station this morning."

"Nonsense," said Mrs. Allen firmly.

"It's true, Mrs. Allen—we have evidence. We captured him."

"You must have made a mistake. Simbele wasn't one of them," she said fiercely.

"He was—we have evidence."

"It's impossible, I tell you; I know him, he's a good man, a teacher."

"We have evidence," the sergeant repeated.

"You are lying," she screamed at him. "You must be lying. Simbele is a good man. I don't care about the terrorists—if they attacked the police station they were mad; but I know Simbele—he's not like that."

"We have evidence," he said again, monotonously.

"It's not true," she shouted again. Then she turned to face Simbele, walked a few paces forward into the open, and looked up at him. "Simbele," she called up, "You didn't do it, did you? What they say you did?"

He made no sign that he heard her.

"Simbele," she called up again. "Simbele, you did not help kill the policemen like they say you did," and when still he made no reply, added, "Did you?"

There was still no sign that he heard. "Simbele," she called. "Please."

He looked up now, looked straight into her face, and even though she was still three yards from him, she could see the weariness in his face. He looked at her, carefully, and then nodded.

"Do you mean that you did help them? You couldn't have. Oh no, you couldn't have."

Simbele, still looking at her, nodded again.

"It's true, you mean," she whispered now, unable to believe. Again he nodded, for the third time, and then she did believe him. Slowly she turned back to Sergeant Van der Post. "What are you going to do to him?" she asked.

"Ask him," the sergeant said, pointing at the white officer on the truck with Simbele.

"What are you going to do to him?" she called up.

He answered her in Afrikaans; she could not understand what he was saying and helplessly interrupted. "I can't understand Afrikaans," she said.

Very deliberately, the officer spat over the side of the truck into the dust at her feet, then said in English. "We are going to make an example of him."

"What do you mean?" asked Mrs. Allen fiercely. "No matter what he has done, no matter how terrible it is, you have no right to do that. If he has committed a crime, you must charge him, you must bring him before a magistrate, you must allow him to see a lawyer."

"You're another one of them, are you?" the policeman said; as if to punctuate his words, the black policeman tugged the rope that was looped around Simbele's neck and Mrs. Allen saw it tighten across his throat and force his head up. The white policeman went on, "You stand with them against us—you are a traitor to your own kind. You are dirty with their dirt," and he pointed at the crowd with his machine-gun.

"You have no right to say that," Mrs. Allen shouted at him.

The policeman bent forward and stared at her, then said, "Let us see then who has the right. Move her away," he told Sergeant Van der Post. He came forward to take Mrs. Allen by the arm; angrily she shook his hand off.

"Move her away, I said," the officer ordered sharply, and the sergeant took her more firmly now, his hands locked on each of her arms, and dragged her back into the crowd—she struggled against his strength, saying, "No, no, leave me alone," but she could not resist, and she was forced back into the crowd.

"Get off," the officer ordered Simbele. The black policeman jerked the rope sharply and Simbele nearly fell; they pushed him to the edge of the truck and then out on to the ground. Then, smiling broadly, the black policeman sat down on the open back of the truck, his feet dangling over the edge, his right hand holding the rope. The officer went forward to the front of the truck and called out over the cab to the crowd in front of the van, "Clear a path there. Come on, quickly, clear a path there." The crowd did not move. "Clear a way there," the officer shouted again, furiously; but still the crowd did not move. The officer jumped over the edge of the truck and strode forward to where the other truck stood; he said something to the sergeant who stood behind the machine gun and then climbed into the cab of the truck, started it, and drove it headlong at the crowd in front, forcing them to leap aside to clear a path; at the edge of the crowd he skidded to a halt, and then reversed the truck down the open path again, and pulled it up parallel to the truck from which he had been speaking. Agilely he leapt out of the cab again and clambered up on to the back of the other truck. Then he leaned over the side and spoke through the window of the cab to the driver. Very slowly the van began to move forward; the rope, that tied Simbele's hands together behind his back, that was then looped around his throat, and that was held at the other end by the black policeman sitting swinging his legs over the back of the truck, slowly tightened, and Simbele was forced to take three or four steps forward. The crowd sighed again and Mrs. Allen, suddenly realizing what was going to happen, began to struggle again against the firm grip of Sergeant Van der Post. The truck drove a little faster now, down through the lane in the crowd that the officer had opened, and Simbele was forced to walk quickly to prevent himself being strangled. By the time the truck reached the edge of the crowd he was running. The truck turned sharply and was driven around the outer edge of the crowd, slowly at first, then faster, with Simbele running desperately to keep up with it. He stumbled and nearly fell, recovered himself, then stumbled again and did fall, was dragged along the ground for a few yards until the officer told the driver to slow down; Simbele got to his feet again, and once again the officer ordered the driver to go forward, to speed up, to slow down after Simbele had fallen again, and then to speed up. The black policeman, sitting on the back of the truck, used the rope as a fisherman uses his line; he slackened it, pulled it taut, slackened it again. Each time the truck circled the crowd, the driver went closer and closer to its edge, forcing the people back, forcing them closer together, until Mrs. Allen and Sergeant Van der Post stood with their backs against the other truck, pressed tight against its sides; and still the truck drove round and round the crowd, with Simbele running behind it, falling, being dragged, struggling up again, running, stumbling, falling, being dragged, once, twice, four times, eight times, until at last he did not try to stand but let himself be dragged through the dust.

The truck stopped now. "Bring the white woman out here," the officer called to Sergeant Van der Post, and she, with her eyes shut, was brought to the edge of the quiet crowd.

"I want you to watch carefully now," the officer said, and, when she did not open her eyes, added, "If you do not watch, I shall go on until you do." She looked up at him now, eyes open and said, "You are . . . you are . . ." and then she found the right word, "You are evil." The officer grinned at her, then turned back to lean over to the driver, and the truck began to move again, forcing Simbele to rise to his feet and to run again. Mrs. Allen watched. After the truck came round for the third time, she said to the sergeant who was still holding her, "Please, sergeant, will you tell him to stop now? They will kill him if they go on any more. Please, I beg you to stop it." Sergeant Van der Post let go of her arms and, as the truck came round again, stepped out into its path to stop it. The driver swung round him and halted, and Sergeant Van der Post said to the officer, "Mrs. Allen says please will you stop now. She begs you to stop."

The officer leaned forward. "Tell Mrs. Allen to ask me herself," and then shouted to the driver to start again. Mrs. Allen threw herself forward and cried up to him, "Please, I beg you, stop now. I beg you to stop, please." The crowd behind her sighed again, like a forest sighs in a sudden small wind.

"If you say please," the officer said, "I shall listen."

"Please," she said helplessly, "Please."

"All right," he said. Then he walked to the back of the truck and looked at Simbele, half-standing, half-crouching there, grey with dust except where the blood washed it away, standing there with his shoulders strangely twisted, standing there panting, looking up, completely silent. "All right, black man," he said to Simbele. "Your white woman has said please. Now you say please—say, Please will you stop now," and then he added, very quietly, "and don't forget to say, Master."

Simbele slowly looked up at him; he said nothing, simply stood there. Fiercely the black policeman tugged the taut rope, forcing Simbele to turn half round, forcing him closer.

"Say, Please stop it, Master," the officer said again.

Now Simbele, in a last effort of strength, turned back against the pressure of the rope; he was only four or five yards away from Mrs. Allen and she could see the blood at his neck where the rope had torn the skin and the sweat that ran through the dust on his face and the dislocated shoulders—and suddenly he pulled with all his might at the rope, throwing himself backwards violently, and the black policeman could not hold the rope and his seat on the truck, and was pulled off down into the dust, letting the rope go as he fell. For a moment or two it seemed that Simbele would try to run, for he took five or six hesitant steps away from the truck, going in the direction of the huts. But then he stopped, turned round again, and facing the crowd, slowly lifted his tied hands above his head and cried out one last great cry, not of defiance, not of rage, but of greeting to his people. Before the crowd could answer, the officer, who had not moved when Simbele tugged the black policeman off the truck except to swing up his sub-machine gun, shot Simbele in the chest and stomach. The cry was still in the air as he fired. Simbele took two paces forward, bending over, almost as if he had been hit from behind, and fell sideways into the dust.

The crowd was silent for a moment, and then sighed again, Mrs. Allen with them. Then she turned to the sergeant and murmured, "How could you? How could anybody be so cruel?"

"He should not have tried to escape."

"He didn't. You murdered him. Deliberately," and now she began to scream, as if what she had seen only now began to affect her. "You murderers. You animals."

"You have no right to say that," said the sergeant fiercely.

"You murderer," she screamed at him.

"So was your friend the black man," said the officer from the back of the truck, and then, as if it justified all objections, went on, "And look at the rest of them now." Mrs. Allen looked round; she had forgotten the crowd around her. They had turned, each person entirely separate, each person on his own, walking back through the dust towards their huts, to their work, not one man, woman or child turning to look back to where Simbele lay curled in the dust. Mrs. Allen took a step or two forward to follow them, then called out, "You can't go. You mustn't go," and the officer called out something to the other white sergeant standing still behind the machine-gun mounted on the other truck, who swung the gun round and up, and fired a burst into the air over the retreating heads; but they did not look round, they did not change their slow pace, they went on walking back to their huts, as if they had heard nothing and seen nothing.

Mrs. Allen stood there watching the retreating crowd until every one of them had disappeared. Then she turned back and watched while the two black policemen picked up Simbele's body by the legs and arms and tossed it carelessly into the back of the truck. She stood there while the policemen got into the trucks and when they roared off through the dust she still stood there. Then she too turned away and walked, slowly through the dust, back to her house.

*   *   *

Old Joseph found her body next morning, lying next to the Allen grave in the cemetery up on the side of the hill, and came cackling down to the settlement to find someone to show it to.

At the inquest, the local doctor gave evidence of how he had been summoned to the camp by the Superintendent after finding the body, of the twelve empty capsules of morphia and the empty 20 c.c. syringe which he had found in her room, and of the injection mark in her thigh. He said that the post-mortem examination had revealed that she died of respiratory failure induced by a large overdose of morphia. He concluded that she had injected herself with about four grains of morphia which she had taken from the dispensary and had then walked up the hill to the cemetery. He reminded the Coroner's Court of the exactly similar circumstances in which Dr. Redman had killed himself; and said that it was remarkable that she had managed to get as far as the cemetery with so much of the drug in her. The Superintendent gave evidence of her previous breakdown and of her strange behaviour since her return to the settlement. Sergeant Van der Post gave evidence of her irrational behaviour at the time of the arrest and shooting of the terrorist Simbele.

The coroner, in giving his verdict, expressed his sympathy for Mrs. Allen's daughter, son-in-law and son, all who were present, and said that Mrs. Allen had obviously taken her own life while temporarily of unsound mind, brought about by her experience when Dr. Redman had committed suicide and by her discovery that a former teacher at the settlement had in reality been a terrorist and by her witnessing of the unfortunate but necessary shooting of the said former teacher.

XV

The settlement is almost deserted now. A few African families still live in some of the less derelict huts and cottages, but most have moved away, to work in the mines, in the factories and on the farms. The Superintendent resigned from the Civil Service and now lives with his nephew and nephew's wife in Bloemfontein; they don't mind having him because he has a decent pension and helps a great deal with the housekeeping. The Department of Bantu Administration decided that it was not worthwhile appointing a successor, since the Church was having difficulty in finding replacements for Dr. Redman and Mrs. Allen—the only application was for the Matron's post and that came from a woman who believed that the Second Coming was so imminent that she had given up everything except prayer—after their experience with Mrs. Allen, the Missionary Committee, advised by the Bishop, thought it best not to appoint her. There was never any question of re-opening the school; for one thing, no one in the region would ever trust a schoolteacher again, for another, there simply were no teachers available. When it became apparent that there was no doctor in all the country prepared to work in that God-forsaken place, the equipment of the hospital was given to the hospital in Verderdorp and Sister Mbele, still mourning for her son, went to work in a mining hospital that had been established in Pietersburg. Even old Joseph died and was buried in a grave that he himself had dug during the weeks before they found him one morning, dead in the little gravedigger's hut on the edge of the cemetery.

So the wind sweeps through the dust and there is nobody to

repair the buildings now; the doors bang and the windows shake and the dust piles high in the corners of the rooms. Old Joseph's hut is falling down and the dust piles high against the gravestones and the wooden crosses. The hot dry winds come sweeping across the valley and the dust piles high against the rocks and stones.

It is not only the settlement that has the look of desolation now, for the whole valley has suffered; most of the farms are deserted and, where the farmers have managed to survive the drought, they have still found it necessary to take jobs in the town and come out only occasionally, to see that the labourers are doing their work. The roads look less used now and nobody bothers to fill in even the worst pot-holes. So, the circles of the not quite hills seem more pronounced, almost as if they were growing to be mountains. The mountains on the perimeter of the valley too seem higher and more wild, and people say that there are still bad men there, waiting out their time.

The towns of the region have suffered too, for nobody chooses to live where there are terrorists who execute ordinary people and where even the police are not immune, though the police have now had a high brick wall built right round the police station, the cells, and the barracks, so that nobody can see in or out—and local people know that they have mounted heavy machine-guns at strategic positions above and inside the high wall. The Town Council of Verderdorp is extremely worried that the management of what few factories there are already there may want to move them to larger and safer towns; but in the Reformed Church they still remember the farmers and policemen whom the terrorists killed and they pray for vengeance; which they shall get, in due time.

The cemetery is still there, of course, perched up on the hill overlooking the derelict settlement. Mrs. Allen is buried next to Dr. Allen, almost in the very spot where her body was discovered for, surprisingly, the Bishop allowed her to be buried in consecrated ground—her children thought that was where she would want to be. The few Africans who still live there don't ever go to the cemetery; they believe that old Joseph haunts the place still—and, certainly, some of his white Barberton daisies have re-seeded themselves, both in his little garden and next to the fallen-down hut, and on Dr. Allen's grave, and you can see them flowering there.

Nobody knows where the police buried Simbele's body.